T0064458

Stoned Clouds

Stoned Clouds

Pratham Padav

PARTRIDGE

A Penguin Random House Company

To order additional copies of this book, contact
Partridge India
000 800 10062 62
orders.india@partridgepublishing.com

www.partridgepublishing.com/india

CONTENTS

PART ONE

WEEKEND PLAN

Saturday was here. Everybody needs a Saturday. Especially those who work for 8 hours from Monday to Saturday. Robin was tired. He hated his job. Saturday is something that he eagerly waited for. He walked out of his office at five past five. He looked at the clouds and took a deep breath.

"Hmmm… finally a Saturday."

He followed his usual schedule. He walked to a nearby kiosk and asked for a lemon tea and a cigarette.

"Lights or Kings?", the shopkeeper asked.

"Lights", he replied.

He drank his tea and smoked his cigarette and he noticed that the shopkeeper was struggling to find change.

"Give me some mint instead."

He put the mint in his mouth and asked for a pack of lights cigarette and started walking home. He found it very weird that the shopkeeper was replying to him in hindi even though he was talking to him in kannada. But then again that's quite common around Bangalore.

As he entered his house he saw his landlord, gave him a fake smile, opened the door and locked it from the inside.

"Thank God I came in before he started talking."

He tears his cigarette pack, makes a roach, removes his weed out of a paper bag, and starts crushing it. Then he removes a paper, puts in the weed, gives it a lick and rolls a joint.

He looks at the mirror and contemplates at the reflection of the joint for a while. Then he looks at his own reflection and says, "I deserve this."

And as he smoked his joint he played some Porcupine Tree music. And his thinking went parallel with the music. He was in deep thought, wondering when he would be going on a trip, when he would be quitting his job, when he would meet the love of his life when suddenly he got a call.

"Hello" whispered Robin.

"Hey, coming to drink?"

"Where?"

"Some new place called GS Bar."

"What? What does GS stand for?"

"Gay Sex"

"What?"

"No, just kidding. Some place called Giraffe Slide Bar."

"What a weird name."

"Who cares? It's got good ratings on the internet."

"Okay, text me the address."

"Will do, see ya."

He puts his phone in his pocket and leaves to meet his friends.

He enters the bar and finds the table where his friends were sitting. Robin didn't have many friends. The three guys who were sitting with him in the table: Alan, Arun and Tanmay were probably his only three friends.

Alan looks at Robin and says, "When I called you, you were stoned, weren't you?"

"Yeah, how did you know?"

"I just know."

As they ordered more and more drinks the conversation went on from life to economy to politics. Robin was zoned out. He was the only guy who didn't participate in any of the conversation. He was in his own world.

"Hey buddy" Arun says staring at Robin's face, "You want to say something."

"About what?"

"What? Were you deaf? Weren't you listening to the discussion."

"No, sorry man. What were you talking about?"

"Prostitution"

"What about it?"

"Oh God, okay let me explain what we were talking about. Apparently I'm the only one who thinks it should be legalized, like completely you know. What do you think retard, give us your opinion."

"Umm… I don't know man, I'm no expert."

"Shut up and say something, you've been silent all night."

"Umm… I guess you know, they should legalize it or not, or maybe they should because prostitution is going to exist regardless of its legal status."

"But don't you think it's immoral", says Alan in a disapproving tone.

Arun looks at Alan and raises his eyebrows and shouts, "Oh shut up Alan! Screw you and screw your morality. Be practical you jackass."

"I think we should order food. I'm hungry." says Tanmay. He wasn't really hungry. He just wanted to change the topic.

After eating and drinking everybody bid goodbye and Robin began to walk home. It was around 12. As Robin looked up he realized that the moon was at the zenith and he could feel a zephyr. It was a full moon night. The streets were walked by tired and intoxicated people. They were all walking in random directions, thought Robin. But then again so was he. While he was walking in a narrow unknown lane he saw something that he found very difficult to register in his mind. He saw a woman. Not just any woman but a beautiful woman. A beautiful woman wearing a white saree and a decent amount of make-up.

Robin still had alcohol flowing in his bloodstream which gave him unanticipated confidence. He walked right towards her trying his best not to fall and not to look like some drunk eve-teaser.

He approaches her and gathers enough wind in his wind pipe and says, "Hello"

"Go away. Don't waste my time." she replied.

Robin realized that this is not going to work and he thought he better be going just when she said…

"The charge is three thousand rupees a night and I'm in no mood to negotiate."

Robin looks up at the moon and then looks around just trying to comprehend the situation.

"Look if you can't afford just walk away." she says in a softer tone.

"Umm… three thousand, uh, okay." he replies in a voice so soft even he couldn't hear himself.

"What?"

"Ah, three thousand okay."

"Okay, follow me, let's go to my room."

She turns around and walks into a dark building and climbs up the stairs. Robin was completely clueless as what would happen in the next few minutes. His thought process was jammed with innumerable thoughts all passing through his mind at the same time. He follows her into a room. And she starts to undress. And he imitates her and undresses himself.

And as she looked at Robin in the eyes who was just sitting there naked on the bed in the most clueless manner she realized that it's his first time.

"Just relax." she said in a comforting tone.

"Okay."

"You don't have to do anything. I'll do everything."

"Okay."

She starts kissing him on every inch of his face and then his neck. Robin closes his eyes and holds her waist firmly with his hands. And she closes her eyes and puts her legs around his waist. He takes a deep breath and begins penetrating her.

He wakes up a few hours later and looks around.

"For some reason this room looks very familiar. Wait a minute… this is my room. So was it all a dream."

He finds his wallet lying next to his face. He picks it up and realizes that there was barely any cash except for a few coins.

And then he realizes that it wasn't a dream but he must have paid her off and walked back home in a drunken state. Which is why he couldn't remember anything except the good part. The best part.

He lifts his neck and stretches his left arm to pick his phone to see the time.

"7.30, hmmm, back to sleep."

PART TWO

THE DREAM AND THE REALITY

He wakes up and sees an old bearded man. It was rather weird because the door was locked.

"Dad?"

"Yes son."

"What are you doing here? How did you get in? And what are you doing with my weed?"

"Just rolling a joint."

"Uh, Okay."

"You got a lighter?"

"I'll light it."

Robin lights his father's joint.

"Hey son, you ever wonder where all this smoke goes."

"Once the smoke is out of your mouth, I guess they just go out. Into the atmosphere or something."

"Yeah, but imagine if the smoke went out our mouths right into the sky. And all the stoners everywhere would blow out the smoke and all that smoke ascends and goes into the sky and all those smoke, the stoned smoke, get together, to form clouds, stoned clouds."

"Interesting theory but also unrealistic."

"There's nothing wrong in dreaming son."

"Really?"

"There's nothing wrong in dreaming as long as you don't forget to wake up."

Robin's vision starts to blur and all of a sudden he blacks out. He could see nothing but darkness. A few minutes later he wakes up.

He goes into the bathroom to brush his teeth. After he finished brushing his teeth and taking a pee he comes back and opens his wallet to look at a passport size photo of an old man with a thick beard. It was a picture of his deceased father.

"What a weird dream, what a weird night."

He goes to the window and looks out. Amidst the clear blue sky there was one cloud.

"I wonder what's directly under that cloud. Hey, it's a Sunday morning and I'm feeling bored. Might as well go out and find out what's under that cloud."

Robin was not really influenced by the dream he had last night where his father spoke of clouds but he wanted to find out what's under the cloud simply and only because he was feeling jobless and didn't have anything better to do that day and he was well aware of that.

He opens the door and goes in search of the mystery that was brewing under that cloud. It was a sunny day and Robin couldn't look up for long as the sky was too bright. But he somehow kept hold of the view of the cloud and went following it. While he was walking a thin road he found a book store.

"Maybe I should buy a book on clouds and weather and stuff. Maybe that'll help me track the cloud better."

So he walked right into the bookstore. It was quite a big bookstore. So he went browsing through the shelves for some random book that he thought would help him track the cloud.

But what he found in the book store was far more amusing than what he expected to find. He saw a woman. Not just any woman but the woman with whom he spent the last night. She was wearing a grey t-shirt and blue jeans and looked like a college student.

He was puzzled. He asked himself, "Why would a well privileged college student be a hooker and what would a hooker be doing in a book store. Hey, maybe she's buying some sex related book that'll help her do her job better. Of course she's buying a sex related book, like duh, she wouldn't be buying a book on quantum physics, right? Or will she? I don't know. Wait, why am I talking to myself? Shut up mind."

And after having a mental argument with himself Robin goes forward to say hi to the woman.

"Hi, I don't know whether you remember me."

She turns around and as soon as she realized that it was her client from last night, she places the book she was holding back in the shelf where it belonged and walked swiftly out of the book store.

"Hmmm… I guess she doesn't remember me."

Robin took out the book she placed back in the shelf.

"Corporate Law?... now why would a…. that's fucking weird."

Robin buys the book in order to read it and understand why that woman would need such a book. He goes home and after some internet research finds out that the book is meant for law students.

"See I told you she was college student." Robin said to himself.

"But wait. That still doesn't explain the hooker thing."

Robin goes to sleep with an unsolved mystery in his head. He wanted to get to the very core of the mystery but he needed sleep. How else would he be able to work the next day.

PART THREE

SIDE EFFECTS OF NOSTALGIA

It was Monday morning again. Robin gets up and follows his usual schedule and heads to his office. He was working as an Analyst at Blue Grass Financial Services. A company that made their employees work from 9 to 5, six days a week. Blue grass was a typical finance company. Located in a tech park, high security, stiff air conditioned air. Robin didn't like the job one bit. But he had bills to pay.

As Robin enters the office he looks at the company name on the reception.

"Blue grass, huh. What the fuck kind of a name is that anyways."

He didn't like anything about the company and the name was no exception.

Since he was working as an analyst he obviously had to do a lot of analysis. One good thing about being an analyst is that you tend to do a lot of analysis and research on each and everything. And Robin intended to use his expertise to find out about one thing and one thing only.… the woman who he fucked.

They say its 8 hours of work but on most days they barely work for 4 to 5 hours and spend the remaining hours trying to figure out how many floors are there in the building and what's new on the cafeteria menu.

Robin didn't want to waste his time like that. He wanted to waste his time 'productively' by researching on that woman.

After half an hour on the internet he finds out that the corporate law book belongs to the syllabus of Karnataka Law University.

"So I guess she's studying there."

He wanted to visit the college wondering whether he would catch a glimpse of her again. But after further research he finds out that the LLB courses there are from Mondays to Saturdays for 3 Hours in the morning i.e 9 to 12. The only way he could make it to that college during class hours was by bunking work.

"Aaa… what's the point. Even if I bunk work and go there what are the chances of me meeting that girl. She might not even be studying there. I don't want to take a risk on a bloody assumption." thought Robin as he mumbled these words staring at the computer screen.

After a while and after some thinking he came to a conclusion: "Ah fuck it, I need a break from this stupid work anyways."

Robin was an expert on faking sicknesses which made it easy for him to get a sick leave on the following Wednesday. He decided to use the sick leave to find her at her college.

As he entered the college campus a wave of memories surged through his mind. His thought process was suddenly jammed with memories of how he spent his three years in college. He felt nostalgic and sad that those days were never going to return when all of a sudden…

"Wait, what the fuck am I thinking. Why the fuck am I feeling nostalgic about those shitty days. Those fucked up days where I had to unproductively waste six hours a day staring at a person whose stupidity was annoying as his authority."

Robin had studied Commerce in a strict Jesuit Institution in a small town outside of Bangalore. His college was like any other college in India; it was run by criminals and politicians. When he was studying in college all he and his friends really wanted was to get out of that prison-like college as soon as possible. But now, that they are out of there some of them really miss college.

When Robin and his friends go out for drinks, one can hear chants such as, "Oh good old days!", "Aaa dinagalu", "Fuck, college life was so simple no?". These were the same friends who used to grumble a lot during college on how badly they wanted to leave college. Robin would get very annoyed by this.

Robin thought about this situation for a while.

"Oh fuck those days dude. Those days are never coming back and I'm glad. Who the fuck wants to go back to college and be treated like slaves by a bunch of impotent retards. I don't want to go back to that time and depend on my stupid parents or listen to a countless meaningless lectures by everyone. I would rather be here than be anywhere else."

Robin was well aware of where he was and what he wanted to be. So when the wave of nostalgic memories surged through his mind he made sure that he stood safely on the shore as he watched the wave breakdown and roll back. He didn't want to drown like the other fools.

He proceeded.

It was around 11 o'clock when Robin had finished roaming all the corridors, peeking inside every class trying to find that one woman who was always difficult to find.

Just when Robin was about to give up he saw something that he was subconsciously hoping for.

A cloud.

A dark one.

"Wait a minute. Could it be?... Could a cloud lead me to her like how it did earlier? Could my dad be right in that dream?"

Robin was staring at the cloud as if he found an oasis in the middle of a desert.

As Robin tried to comprehend the reason for the existence of that one dark cloud he realized that there were many more dark clouds forming around it.

"Wait, what the hell."

It began to rain.

With no hope left to spare Robin decided to call it a day and head back home.

PART FOUR

THE LINE OF ARGUMENT

As Robin began to travel back home with the weight of shame above his shoulders he got a call from good ol' Arun.

"Dude, are you coming to drink later?" shouts Arun.

"Yeah sure, when?"

"At around 6."

"Why don't we catch up for a drink right now."

"Dude, I'm at work, everybody will be working right now, how can we drink now? Wait, aren't you in the office?"

"Oh, never mind, we'll meet up later. But where?"

"Same place."

And with that phone call Robin was scheduled for yet another heavy drinking session. Robin was desperate to drink considering his failure in his recent endeavor.

Robin was the first to arrive at the bar.

As soon as Arun saw Robin he yelled, "Dude, how come you came so early man? Usually you're the last to arrive."

"Yeah, I guess, who cares. Just order your drinks."

As time passed by Alan and Tanmay joined as well.

Alan opens his big mouth and says, "What a fucked up day. The workload is getting too hectic. I wish I go back to college."

"Oh fuck. Why God why?" moaned Robin.

"What? What happened?" enquired Alan.

"Nothing man, whatever." replied Robin.

And Alan continued: "It was so chilled out when we were in college, no? Now it's so fucked up man. I wish I could go back to college man."

To which Tanmay said, "Ya man, good old days."

And Robin said, "Oh fuck. Can someone please shoot me right now."

At this point Alan and Tanmay looked really confused.

"Why man, what happened?" asked Alan.

"Ya man, how much did you drink." asked Tanmay.

"I'm not drunk, I'm alright. The only people who are fucked in their heads are you guys." replied Robin.

Sudden silence.

Awkward silence.

Confusion.

"Excuse me sir, could you get us one plate chicken 65." said Tanmay pointing his finger at the waiter who at this point had become an expert on avoiding awkward and intense moments.

Alan was confused and annoyed at the things that were coming out of Robin's mouth.

"Dude seriously, what's up with you?" asked Alan in an interrogating manner.

"Nothing man. I just get mindfucked when you guys talk about college."

"What, why?"

"Because college sucked. I mean what is wrong with you guys. We had to go there everyday to get treated like shit by the principal, vice principal, dean, the management, the lecturers, even the fucking watchman. Do you remember the time we all got kicked out of class because none of us had shaved our goatees?"

"Ya man, I remember." says Alan, "Those were fun times."

"FUN TIMES? Fun times you say? Are you fucking kidding me? Some bitch forced us to shave an integral part of our body. That is a fucking human right violation right there. You just got abused of your human rights. We had to shave of our faces so that some whore could be at peace. But hey, hey, hey, who cares, those were FUN TIMES, right?"

Alan sweats a little on his forehead, sucks his saliva down his throat and gathers enough voice in sound pipe and says, "Chill dude, you don't have to get so emotional."

"EMOOOOOTIONALLL! Holy fuck!" said Robin and took a long deep breath, "Don't do this Alan, Don't fucking do this."

"Don't fucking do what?" asked Alan.

"Don't feed my impulse to take this beer bottle and hit you on your head." replied Robin angrily.

"I'm gonna go take a pee. Does anyone want to come?" asked Tanmay trying to derail the train of argument.

"No man, you go. We have an issue to resolve." replied Alan.

So Tanmay goes alone to the restroom away from all the tension and heat.

Alan was very persistent to win this argument.

"You say what you want to say man. But most of us miss our college days and it's quite normal. Just because you're abnormal, just because you had a bad time in college, that doesn't give you the right to expect others not to miss their college days." explained Alan.

"You were right about one thing though." said Robin nodding his head.

"What?"

"I am abnormal."

"That wasn't really a compliment."

"Thank you though. You know what I never understood about the 'shave-your-beard' rule"

"Oh no! Not again. You don't have to drag that topic so much."

"No, no, listen. We were studying in a Jesuit College, right?"

"Ya"

"Now I really don't understand why they asked us to shave our beard or goatee or whatever when the Jesuits there worship Jesus, who by the way had a handsome beard. They have no problem worshipping a man with a beard but when it comes to us they say, 'please come neatly to college, please come clean shaven as we don't want to you look like a bunch of rowdies', what are they trying to imply from that. What a bunch of hypocrites!"

Now that was a good line of argument.

And Alan had realized that he had no comeback for that and he said what every individual who knows they're going to lose an argument would say, "Okay man. You only! I'm wrong, everybody is wrong, the whole world is wrong, only you're right. Happy?"

At this point Arun who was silent the entire session pitches in and says, "Okay guys, let's not argue about something that happened one billion years ago. I think it's time to go."

Tanmay returns from the restroom and says, "Ya guys lets go. I need to pee."

"What? Didn't you just go to the restroom", asked Alan.

"Ya but I couldn't pee there, someone has puked all over the restroom floor." replied Tanmay.

"Okay now we definitely need to leave." said Arun who also needed to pee.

PART FIVE

SUPERFICIAL DIM BRAINS

All four of them were out of the bar. Arun and Tanmay started their motorbikes and headed home quickly as they both wanted to visit the bathroom as soon as possible. Alan took a rickshaw and headed back home.

Robin was all alone walking on the sidewalk with a cigarette in his mouth. He talks to himself whenever he is alone. He preferred talking to himself more than talking with normal people. He knew people were dim and superficial. He was aware that he was living in a world where people valued their personal opinions more than they valued facts. He was aware that in most cases facts are contrary to popular opinion.

He wasn't fond of having talks with his friends or relatives, with his parents or cousins. Robin had a feeling that they were all 'Knowledge Anorexic'. Some people don't eat because they're afraid of becoming fat and some people don't learn because they're afraid that someday they'll become smart and realize how dumb and wrong they used to be once upon a time. Robin always thought that people had developed anorexia towards knowledge.

"How else could people be so dumb?" thought Robin.

"Ha, people and their superficial dim brains. I wonder when they'll start thinking deeper."

As Robin thought about such dim issues the light from the night-sky got dim as well.

Robin looked up and saw a dark cloud that began to cover the moon.

"Oh no! I hope it doesn't rain again."

As Robin walked forward looking up at the sky he bumped into a person.

"Oh I'm so sorry, I didn't mean to…." said Robin whose speech had suddenly halted.

PART SIX

TSUNAMI

The person who Robin bumped into looked familiar.

"Wait a minute, I know you." said Robin in an exciting tone.

It was her.

Robin looked up and thanked the cloud.

But she began to walk away.

"Wait." said Robin.

"What?" she replied.

Robin knew he had to say something smart to stop her from running away, so he said the diplomatic thing he could have thought of.

"I have three grand."

"Okay." she replied, "Follow me."

And once again Robin was led into a dark building where he walked on stairs that were beyond his visibility. His thought process was once again jammed with innumerable thoughts all passing through his mind at the same time.

The nostalgic feeling that went going through Robin's mind earlier that day was just a wave. He stood safely on the shore and survived that wave. But this was no wave. It was a Tsunami. A tsunami that almost paralyzed his mind.

They entered the room.

For the next few hours Robin was in heaven. His thought process which was previously jammed with innumerable thoughts was now committed to just one thought. The only thing he could think of was her.

He felt like a hedonist whose pleasure was increasing by the second. He felt like a nomad because for the first time in his life he forgot who he was and where he was going.

The only thing he could think of was her; the smell of her hair, the taste of her skin and the heat of her blood kept his mind occupied and his body too.

His heart was pumping so fast that he could feel his ribs vibrate out of his chest. He could feel his blood vessels heat up due to the speed at which his heart was pumping blood to the body.

After a few hours they stopped. His nerves began to calm. His body began to cool down.

Robin drank a sip of water from a clay pot that placed on the side of bed. He then went to the corner of the room and lit his cigarette. And so did she.

Robin finished his cigarette and chucked it in the ashtray.

There was silence and calmness for the next five minutes.

"Wanna grab some breakfast?" asked Robin who couldn't think of any other thing to say.

"Sure. My treat." she replied.

"How come?"

"I'll tell you while we're having breakfast."

PART SEVEN

BREAKFAST

They kept walking, trying to find a nice place to eat. They walked for around fifteen minutes. As they reached the main road they found a nice little café that sold hot cheesecakes, lemon tea along with a few other south Indian dishes.

They entered the café and ordered their food. They didn't utter a word for the first 10 minutes.

Gradually Robin broke the ice, "What's your name?" he asked.

"Ha." she replied as her lips curved to form a smile.

"No really, What's your name?"

"Asha"

"That's a nice name. Easy to pronounce, easy to remember. Is that why you chose that name as your alias?"

"Hahaha, you're very funny. What's your name?"

"Robin"

"Easy to pronounce, easy to reme…"

"But that's my real name."

"Good for you. Unfortunately some of us need to keep an alias."

"Your English is impeccable. You seem to be highly educated. Why'd you choose to be like this?"

"Hey, listen asshole. My way of life is none of your business. I came to have breakfast with you just to be polite. Not to get interrogated."

"Uh, wait, wait, hold on. Don't misunderstand. I'm sorry if I'm asking too many questions. It's just that you're the most interesting person I've ever met. I didn't mean to offend you in any way."

"Of course I'm the most interesting person you've ever met. How often do you find a scholar hooker roaming in and around the streets of Bangalore."

"Yeah, you're right."

"But you're a loser. Aren't you?"

"What?"

"You were a probably a virgin before you met me. You're probably one of those techies who work in some bloody techpark at odd hours and make enough money to pay rent for a small one bedroom house. You probably have like 2 or 3 friends and all of them are boring losers just like you or worse."

"Look who's interrogating now?"

"Ya, you caught me there."

"You guessed almost everything right about me."

"Almost, eh? I guess I'll have to try again some other time. But now I guess I'll have to leave."

"Leave? So early?"

"Ya. Some of us have very busy lives you know."

"Wait, you still didn't tell me why you're treating me."

"I don't know, just like that."

"You've no reason to be a hooker. You've no reason to treat me. Yet you do it. Do you realize that you're an extremely unreasonable person."

"Ya I guess. It's time to leave. Let's go."

And they both walked out of the café. They said their goodbyes and when she was about to get inside a rickshaw Robin yelled, "Wait, how will we meet again?"

She turned around and handed him a small card before she left.

"Wow, thanks Asha."

"Call me only when you mean business. Not for breakfasts or meaningless chats, okay?"

"Got it." replied Robin.

As Robin stood there contemplating the card he suddenly realized that it was the middle of the week.

"Shit………. office."

PART EIGHT

THE VOICE INSIDE MY HEAD

Robin walked into his office. He reached the door where he needed to flash his ID card on the machine before he enters. He flashed the card and the machine didn't make any sound. Usually the machine makes a beeping tone. He tries again and there's still no sound. The security guard was getting a little suspicious.

"Oh shit."

The card Robin was flashing was not his ID card but the card that Asha had given him.

Robin put that card inside and removed out his ID card, flashes it and enters.

For the next few days Robin's mind was occupied with only one thing- Asha.

He wanted to know everything about her. Where she's from, what she does, how did she end up here, everything. And now that he had her number he knew he could meet her more often. And he did.

Almost every weekend he would give her a call and spend all his savings on an expensive pursuit. He knew he was spending way too much money but the voice inside his head wouldn't listen. At the end of every session he would ask her a few questions about her and she would try to dodge them. Gradually, she would give in and answer a few of them. They both knew that they were getting quite close to each other but Asha had other clients too. So once in a while she would use that as an excuse not to attend Robin in order to avoid having a close relationship with him. She didn't want to mix business with pleasure. But little did she know that in the business of pleasure anything is possible.

Robin was disappointed because Asha wouldn't pick up his calls. But there's nothing much he could do. So he spent the weekend all alone at home. He downed a few beers, smoked a fat joint and went to sleep.

When he woke up a he saw a familiar face.

"Dad?"

"Nice to see you again, son."

"Dad, I thought you were dead."

"I am."

"Then how are you standing here…. in front of me?"

"Ha."

"What?"

"So did you find out?"

"Find out what?"

"Find out what's under the cloud?"

"Oh, well, I did find something."

"What did you find son?"

"A woman."

"You found a woman?"

"Yes dad."

"That's it?"

"Wait, what? Are you telling me that there's more?"

"The cloud floats above the surface, the surface on which people walk. The cloud floats above the surface, the surface on which people build, live, work, fight, kill, eat, sleep and shit. There are a lot of things underneath that dark cloud. The cloud sees everything but you don't. Try to find out what's under the cloud. Try to find out what the cloud sees. The cloud knows everything."

"But, why? I don't want to know everything."

"Who's asking you to know everything? It's not possible to know everything. I'm just saying that if you try to know what the cloud sees you'll know a bit more than what you know now. Isn't that a good thing?"

"Ya, but I've got work and friends and a lot of other stuff to do. I don't have time for that cloud."

"You go to the office and you listen to your bosses, you go out and listen to your friends. Do you like listening to them?"

"Uh.... no."

"There is only one thing that you're supposed to listen."

"And what's that?"

"The voice inside your head."

"What?"

"The voice inside your head. The noise that vibrates within the walls of your skull. Listen to it son. What does the voice inside your head tell you?"

"Follow the cloud."

PART NINE

THE CONVENTIONAL LOSER

Alan wakes up to his phone alarm. He shuts it down and begins his day. He goes to the bathroom and stares at the mirror. And with a frown on his face, he brushes his teeth. He says his morning prayers and stares at the breakfast in his plate. He curses the world for a minute and then begins to eat his breakfast.

Alan was a cynic. A pessimist. His parents had three sons. And he was their third favorite son. He was an obedient son. He studied engineering, not because he wanted to but because his parents wanted him to. And now he's doing what most engineers in this country do. He works in a call centre.

He hates his life. He hates his work. He hates the world.

He was a dim guy. He was bullied from primary school to engineering college. He was also quite narrow minded.

He spends half his free time watching porn. What else could the poor fucker do? He was 26 years old and he could barely speak to a girl. And even if he did approach a girl she would probably just walk away. He didn't have much of a look. He was short and skinny. He was balding in the front. He had a terrible posture and would slouch while walking. This poor guy was neither blessed with good looks, confidence nor a sense of humor.

On one fine day he gets a call from his Cousin Jude.

"Hey bro, what's up ra?" shouted Cousin Jude.

"Nothing much man." Replied Alan.

"Wanna come to a party?"

Cousin Jude was a ladies man. He was rich, he had the looks, he was cocky and he helped run his dad's business. Every uncle and aunty loved Jude. Cousin Jude was an exact antonym to Cousin Alan.

"Ah? I don't know man." replied Alan.

"Come man, anyways you sit at home and do nothing. Might as well come here."

"But what will I do there?"

"It's a party da. Come and drink, smoke and mingle and all ra."

"Ummm... Okay."

Alan dressed up to leave for Cousin Jude's party.

Cousin Jude lived in big house in one of the finest neighborhoods of Bangalore.

The crowd was young and so was the night.

Women at that party never looked more beautiful and men never more that high.

When Alan arrived at the party he noticed one thing. Everybody was with somebody. Except for him.

He headed straight to the bar and began gulping in a desperate attempt to drown his loneliness.

Out of nowhere came Cousin Jude who patted him in the back.

"Having a great time, eh?" asked Cousin Jude.

"Ya man, nice party."

"What are you doing here sitting alone? Come with me. I'll introduce you to some ladies."

Cousin Jude dragged him with his arms around his shoulders and introduced him to some of his friends. Unfortunately none of them were interested in him.

While they were all talking he was just standing in the corner, nodding his head at everything.

In the end he realized its best he heads back to the bar. After a few drinks he gained a little confidence. He approached a few girls and tried breaking the ice. But sadly, everytime he broke the ice he would sink in to the freezing waters and freeze himself. Not a single girl Alan saw that day even glanced at him. Alan tried talking to them but in return he would get the 'Go away' look from those girls' faces.

Left with no other choice he headed back to the bar.

While he was sitting in the bar he noticed a guy drinking next to him who had a baby face.

"Woah bro, aren't you supposed in school or something?" asked Alan.

"Piss off man." replied the kid in return.

Alan kept his mouth shut.

After a while the kid looked at Alan and asked, "Are you having a bad time?"

"Yeah, why?"

"Do you want to have a good time?"

"What do you mean?"

"If you were on what I am right now, you'd be having great time."

"What are you on?"

"Ecstasy"

"What? How old are you?"

"I'm older than you think. I'm 17."

"Well, that's not old enough."

"Why do you care? Do you want it or not?"

Alan thought for a while. When he reflected on his current state of affairs he realized that he desperately needed something that would change the situation.

"How much?" asked Alan.

"One grand."

"Too much."

"Okay buh-bye."

"No, no, no, no, wait. Fine, fine. One grand it is."

"Come with me."

The kid took Alan behind the house and gave him the stuff. Likewise Alan gave him the money.

Alan went back inside the house and headed straight to the bathroom. He removed the tablet out, put it in his mouth and swallowed it. He then looked into the mirror and stared at the reflection of his eye in the mirror and then deeper into the reflection of his body in his eye in the mirror.

He couldn't stare anymore as the sweat from his forehead began dripping down his eyebrows.

He could feel his heart beat faster. He could hear his heart beat like an orchestra drum. He felt like an alpha wolf on a full moon night.

He ran out of the bathroom and went straight to the bar. He began drinking a pint of beer to quench his thirst. The bartender was a bit confused as to why this man had switched from whisky to beer.

Alan could feel his nerves vibrate out of his skin. He could feel his consciousness float and his mind fly.

In one hand Alan was holding the beer bottle and with his other hand he was holding his jaw which was vibrating with the beats of the music.

Within a blink of an eye he was on the dance floor trying to comprehend the situation that he was rowing in.

He could feel the music turning his brain inside out.

"Since when did music sound so good, God I think I'm in heaven. Fuck, I need to dance."

Alan danced alone on the dance floor until the drug began to wear off.

When the euphoric effects began to wear off, Alan looked around at the beautiful women.

"Man, I never thought women could look so beautiful. Fuck, I need to have sex."

Alan wanted to be with a woman at any cause. But he knew one thing for sure.

"I have no chance with these girls."

He had no chance with those girls. In fact, he had no chance with any girl. But he was desperate.

Suddenly Alan noticed a familiar face moving around the corner of the room.

It was the same kid who sold him the drug. Alan swiftly walked right at the boy.

"Dude, I need some more."

The kid was stuck.

"Need more what?"

"The stuff that you sold me."

"Oh, I'm out of that man."

"Fuck, Fuck, Fuck."

"Dude, hold it together man. Stop flipping."

"Dude I'm so fucking horny right now. I need either a drug or a woman right now."

"I think can arrange that."

"Oh cool, you got more drugs."

"Nope" replied the kid.

"Woman?" asked Alan curiously.

"A friend of a friend of mine gave me a number of some call girl. I never used that number but I think you could have some use for it right now."

"What? A prostitute?"

"Yeah man, what's wrong?"

"Fuck, fuck. Alright just give me the number."

"Okay here you go."

The kid gives him the number and walks away.

Although Alan was a devout catholic, he didn't care at the moment that he was about to do something that he considered an abomination.

He picks out his phone from his pocket and dials in the number.

The phone begins to ring for a long time but is left unpicked. Just when Alan thought of cutting the call someone picks up the call.

Alan could hear nothing from the other side except the sound of someone breathing heavily.

Alan gathers enough air in lungs and says, "Hello.... who's this?"

"Asha"

PART TEN

CONFLICTING EXPERIENCES

After another dirty weekend the boys were at the bar. Robin had recently received a bonus, so he was paying the bill that night. However, he didn't tell his friends why he was treating them because he didn't want to disclose the fact that he had received a bonus, because if he did they would ask for more treats. And his friends never bothered to ask Robin why he was treating them because they cared more for free booze than the reason behind it.

It took them no time to get drunk. As more and more alcohol began to flow through their bloodstreams, the conversations they were having began to heat up. The conversation degraded to arguments which covered subjects such as life, work, sex, drugs, politics, religion, illuminati and every other thing that an average 20s male would talk about to make himself feel more important.

"What's wrong with sex, ah? Nothing ah? What's wrong with money, ah? Nothing ah?" yelled Robin.

"What are you trying to say?" asked Alan.

"Then what's wrong with sex for money. It should be completely okay then right?" asked Robin again.

"What the fuck are you saying man. Are you trying to advocate prostitution now? That's disgusting." replied Alan.

"Which part the sex or the money?" asked Robin.

"It's not the sex or the money. It's the sex and the money that disgusts me. Prostitution is sick, illegal and unholy."

"Look around man, almost everything we do is sick, illegal and unholy."

"Doesn't matter. Prostitution is sick. Those whores should be arrested and thrown away so that they don't spread their filthy fucking diseases."

"Who knows man, hookers may be normal people just like you and me. They can be nice people too I guess."

"How the fuck would you know that. You're talking like you've been hanging around with a prostitute."

At this point Robin was feeling a bit nervous as he was in fact hanging around with a prostitute.

"Umm…. Ahh, hey how would um, how would you know that a prostitute is filthy or whatever. You're talking like you've been hanging around with a prostitute." replied Robin.

At this point Alan was getting a bit nervous because he had spent the last weekend with a prostitute.

"Ah… well I know that because you know, I watch TV man. And I see shit like this everyday on the news."

"But Alan, you need to get laid with a hooker man."

"What? Why?"

"Because that's the only way you can ever get laid."

The whole gang starts laughing at Alan.

"Well I can get laid alright." replies Alan in a defensive tone.

"With who? Your mom?"

At this point the gang burst into a roar of laughter.

"Hey asshole. You don't have to bring my mom in between."

"I couldn't bring your mom in between even if I wanted to. She's as fat as a pregnant cow."

At this point Alan wanted to murder Robin. While everyone was laughing Alan was just sitting silently in the corner, drinking his drink and smoking his cigarette.

In the end Robin paid the bill and everyone left. Arun and Tanmay were the first to leave and Robin walked on the dark street alone. Alan found an empty beer bottle lying on the footpath right outside the bar and he picked it up and thought, "Ah finally. Now that Robin is walking alone, maybe I should just beat that fucker up and teach him a lesson for good."

As Alan followed Robin in the dark alley he suddenly notices something shining. Something so bright that it lit that dark alley. Something so bright that it was almost God-like.

"Jesus Christ, who is that?"

Alan's mind was numb when he realized who it was.

"Fuck, I know that woman."

Alan wanted a closer look, so he went ahead and stood behind a parked car.

"What? What's happening? What's that moron doing with my hooker?"

As Alan tried processing thoughts into his curious mind, he saw Robin and Asha walk into a pub. He realized that he can't walk into the pub, because if he did they would definitely notice him.

Alan had no choice but to just stand there and let his curious mind make assumptions. An empty mind is like a grave hole. If you don't fill a grave hole with a dead body it's eventually going to be filled with dirt or grass or whatever. But it is going to be filled. Similarly Alan was in possession of an empty curious mind. He couldn't fill it with facts because he couldn't get any. So he filled it with assumptions.

"Why would someone take a prostitute to a pub? A normal person would just fuck them. Maybe he works with her. Maybe he's her pimp or some associate or whatever. Oh fuck. Maybe that's how he got the money to treat us today. Maybe that's why the bastard didn't tell us why he's treating us. Fuck. Holy fuck. That son of a bitch. No wonder he defends prostitution. That piece of filthy shit. I wonder how much money he's making."

Alan lit a cigarette, took a long drag. He thought for a while. Then he caught a rickshaw and went home.

PART ELEVEN

THE LAST GENERATION ENTREPRENEUR

He fucked her. He fucked her hard. He felt no empathy. He used his women for pleasure. Once he was done fucking them, he would use them as an ashtray. He would light his cigarette and chuck the ash on his hookers. Everybody in the neighborhood feared him.

His name was Rajan.

He ran the local prostitute business along with the local drug trafficking business. The cops knew what he was doing but wouldn't say or do anything.

Anything illegal that was bought or sold around; heroin, cocaine, hash, sex, had to go under his supervision. And he always made money out of it.

The local peddlers and hookers had to give him a part of their profit and a part of their service in order to survive.

The criminal business was a dying business. It was not the 90s anymore when it was a striving business. Now there are plenty of companies with new jobs opening their doors to youngsters. The youth is more educated and employed. Not many youngsters want to be a rowdy anymore. Therefore it had become difficult for criminal mobs like Rajan to hire people. And to make things worse the rise of the media had made it even more difficult to keep confidential criminal businesses confidential. It was a dying culture. An ending era. Rajan had no successor. He was the last one. He was standing at the end of a long horizon. An empire would fall at his demise. Never to rise again. He was a last generation entrepreneur.

"How are my girls doing? Are they reaping good profits?" asked Rajan to one of his subordinates.

"Yes sir, they're doing very well, except for a few."

"Who are these few? I need to make money. You know that right? The cops and politicians nowadays, they don't come cheap. Their bribe rates are going up. So tell me who are these 'few'?"

"The old ones, some of our aging prostitutes, they don't make money like they used to."

"Of course they don't. Assets depreciate. I'm aware of that. Then? Who else?"

"Well some of them are distracted."

"Like?"

"Asha"

"Oh the star player. The man of the match, oh wait the woman of the match. That angel used to make us a lot of money. What happened to her?"

"She's distracted boss."

"Distracted, ah? What distraction?"

"Some guy"

"Oh love, love, love. Crazy old love. Say boy, do you know the story of sleeping beauty?"

"Ah, yes boss. I do"

"What happens in the end?"

"The sleeping beauty never wakes up. So some handsome guy comes and kisses her, then she finally wakes up."

"Oh that's the version that you heard. Do you know the original version?"

"Original version?"

"Oh yes, the original version. In which the handsome prince tries to wake the sleeping beauty and gives up. Then he rapes her and she wakes up a few months later to the pain of childbirth. The original story was all about murder, rape, terror and cannibalism. Of course the cartoon movies changed the story here and there because if they didn't, we would be living in a society where there would be a lot of kids aspiring to be rapists. Oh wait a minute, that wouldn't make much difference now, would it, because a lot kids are growing up to be rapists anyways. Haaaaa….. everything they told us when we were kids were nothing but lies. Love itself is a lie. All those stories and tales are all bullshit. Anyways about Asha… well what do I usually do to a threat?"

"Sir, usually if someone was a threat or caused you a problem you would order us to cut off their head and dump it in the garbage. Do you want us to cut off Asha?"

"You idiot. You complete idiot. Don't be a fool. When someone steals your eggs you don't need to kill the chicken, you need to kill the thief."

"So what do we do boss?"

"Don't kill the girl, kill her distraction. Go find who this boy is. Cut off his head and then dump it somewhere."

"Yes sir."

"Once you kill the boy my chicken will give me more eggs like it used to. Now, go make me an omelet."

"Okay boss."

PART TWELVE

AN UNCONVENTIONAL END TO THE CONVENTIONAL LOSER

"That fucking bastard. That fucking rich pimp bastard. That Robin is probably a fucking millionaire. God knows how many prostitutes work for him. I need to get a piece of him." shouts Alan staring at a mirror in his bedroom.

Alan had been drinking too much in the past few days. Some of his cousins who were the same age as him were now married. But he still didn't have a girlfriend. Alan knew that having a lot of money could change his life drastically.

"The best way to make easy money is by doing something illegal. Like what that bastard Robin is doing."

Suddenly his phone starts beeping.

"Bro, Tanmay here."

"Ya, tell me."

"Coming out?"

"Sure, who all are coming?"

"Usual"

"Okay, I'll come in some time."

Alan puts the phone in his pocket and stares at the mirror and says, "You're already fucking drunk, what are going to do going there."

After a while Alan shouts, "Oh… Robin is going to be there. Since I'm going there I might as well ask that fucking bastard for some financial advice on how to get rich quick with help from a few sluts."

And with that in mind Alan dressed up to leave to the bar.

As usual the gang was there and it took them no time to get drunk. And as usual they got into deep discussions ranging from friendship, life, work, death, politics, sex and whatever else came into their minds.

Alan, on the other hand was silent. He didn't utter a word. Because he knew that if he opened his mouth he would ask Robin about his latest endeavors, about money and sluts. So he kept his mouth shut. He had a deep need to open his mouth and ask Robin everything, but he resisted. He resisted for good.

After a while Robin got up and went to the loo. But he left his phone on his chair. While he was in the loo squeezing his seed his phone started beeping.

Alan noticed that and picked up his phone. It was a text message. He opened the text message.

The message said:

"Asha: Need 2 meet u ryt nw!!"

"Holy fuck." thought Alan.

He deleted the message and kept Robin's phone back unnoticed.

All sorts of thoughts were going through Alan's mind.

Once again Robin's phone beeped. And Alan did the same. This time the message gave an address of an old warehouse where Asha wanted to meet up. And once again Robin read the text, deleted it and kept it back in its place unnoticed.

Alan had drowned himself in an ocean of thoughts.

"Maybe its pay day for Robin. That slut is probably calling him to pay him the pimp's cut. But what if I show up there instead of Alan and take away all the money. I'll be fucking rich." thought Alan in his drunken state.

Robin came back from the loo and picked up his phone only to see that there are no new messages.

After the drunken rendezvous ended Alan decided to go to the old warehouse all by himself with a goal in his mind. The goal of cashing in.

He took a rickshaw and headed to the destination. He got out of the rickshaw, paid the driver and walked alone in a dark lane. At the end of the lane stood an old dusty brown warehouse. Nobody was there.

"I hope I've not reached the wrong address."

Alan looked around for a while and reached the entrance of the warehouse. He saw a few men standing by the entrance of the warehouse. He walked by the entrance and before he could say a word one of the men asked, "Are you Robin?"

"Um, yeah, Robin, well that's me. That's me. I'm Robin." answered Alan.

"We've been waiting for you."

"Good, good. So, where's the money."

"What?"

"You know? The fucking money. Robin's cut. Ah, my cut."

"Uh, its inside."

The men escorted Alan who was playing Robin into the warehouse.

"Okay so where's my money?" ordered Alan.

"You're the guy who's been spending too much time with Asha, right? asked a bearded man.

"Yup that's me. Now where's my cut? Where's the pimp's cut?"

"What the fuck is he talking about?" shouts the bearded man looking at the other standing there.

The men there were confused as to what Alan was shouting. After a while the leader of the gang says, "You know what, let's not wait anymore. Let's get the work done as ordered."

One of the men removed a long machete out of a black bag while the other men put Alan on the floor and started kicking him.

"What the fuck is going on? Please leave me alone. I don't know anything. I'm not even Robin. Robin is my fucking bastard friend. Please. You've got to trust me."

"Shut up you lying bastard. You've had your fun. Now it's time to die." shouts a man placing the machete on Alan's neck.

And with a single strike a life came to an end. A consciousness ceased to exist. The life of a conventional loser met an unconventional end. A zillion memories faded to black in a few milliseconds. A departed soul. A lifeless body. More like a headless body. This was the state of Alan.

The gang leader drops the bleeding machete and picks up his ringing phone.

"Hello Rajanna" he said with pride.

"Hello, is the job done?"

"Ah, yes the boy he came to the warehouse and started talking about some money and…."

"Shut up. I don't care how you did it. But did you do it?"

"Yes boss. The boy is dead."

"Good, finish the ritual. Dump his filthy head where it belongs. Dump it in the largest pile of garbage you can find in this town."

"Yes boss."

PART THIRTEEN

THE MARWADI HIPPY AND HIS MAGICAL CAMEL

"I wish I could travel around the world." exclaimed Robin sitting alone in his room.

"I wish I could meet new people, eat new food, learn new languages and live different cultures. Why does my life have to be so stale? I wish I could quit my job and go out there and explore."

And suddenly he could hear his phone ring. It was Arun.

"Stoned?" asked Arun.

"Ya, how'd you know?"

"Wanna get more stoned? I'm home alone."

"Ya sure."

Robin put on some clothes marched towards Arun's place.

There was Arun and Tanmay waiting for him with their eyes as red as the Satan's horns.

"Where's our hero?" asked Robin.

"Who? Alan? We tried calling him but he didn't pick up." replied Tanmay.

"He's probably jacking off." said Robin.

"Okay boys, time to get stoned." shouted Arun rolling a fat one.

And after smoking a few joints they were all really hungry.

"I think we better order some food to be delivered." suggested Tanmay.

"No, no, no, no, no, no, no." squeaked Robin.

"Why not?" moaned hungry Tanmay.

"Today we should do something new. Something we've never done before."

"Dude, we're hungry man. Don't fuck with us."

"No Tanmay, just chill. We'll eat something new man. I'm in a mood to do something new."

"Whatever man, as long as we get to eat."

"What's on your mind?" asked Arun.

"How about some camel meat? I've never tried it before." said Robin.

"Neither have I." replied Arun.

"Neither have any of us. But where do we get it?" asked Tanmay desperately, "I'm really hungry man. Tell quickly."

"Alright chill out man. I heard we get it in Cox Town." said Robin in an unconvincing tone.

"You heard? Which means you're not sure? Dude, I'm fucking hungry." yelled Tanmay rubbing his tummy.

"Dude, c'mon man. It'll be like an adventure. Like a stoned adventure."

"You know what? He's actually got a point. Let's get in my car and go searching for camel meat." said Arun picking up his car keys.

Left with no other choice all Tanmay could say was "Oh fuck. It better taste good man."

And they all hopped into Arun's little car for a drive that would take at least half an hour away from their lives.

"Dude I'm thirsty man. If not to eat, at least can we stop somewhere for a drink" cried out Tanmay.

And so they stopped at a bar near Frazer Town which was on the way. They bought a bottle of whisky, three bottles of water, some plastic cups and of course some cigarettes.

While driving to Cox Town Arun was sipping from the whisky bottle.

"I thought we're not supposed to drink and drive." asked Robin who was sitting next to him.

"I thought you wanted to do something new and adventurous. Now I'm giving you an adventure. So shut up and be thankful bitch." replied Arun as he turned the steering wheel.

"Yes sir. Whatever you say. Let's get some camel meat." said Robin who was really excited.

They finally reached Cox Town.

Arun stopped his car under a tree's shade.

"What now?" asked Tanmay, "Cos I'm really hungry."

"Relax, it has to be somewhere around here." replied Robin.

"You mean…. you mean you don't know where it is?" screamed Tanmay.

"Dude stop screaming, let me think." replied Robin.

"Ya, let him think man." said Arun taking Robin's side.

"Whatever man, I'm getting out." said Tanmay as he got out of the car.

"Hey, if you're going to the bar take this money and buy another bottle. We need a refill." said Arun who was already smashed.

Tanmay came back from the bar and gets into the car with one and a half bottle of whisky, 2 packets of chips and some fried chicken covered in an aluminum foil. And of course some cigarettes.

"I'm not sharing my food with you lousy bastards." yelled Tanmay.

"At least give us our booze." said Arun to which Tanmay handed him a bottle.

"Did you guys figure out where the camel meat is, yet?" asked Tanmay impatiently.

"I think it's over there, or this way or somewhere near MM Road." replied Robin.

"Fuck this, you know what? Let's just go driving around. Maybe then we'll know where it is." said Arun starting his engine.

They went up and down the flyover. They went on the same road a couple of times. They pretty much covered up

Cox Town and Frazer Town entirely. They had finished a few bottles of whisky and smoked some joints to go with it. But with no food in their stomachs Robin and Arun were starving.

"Dude I give up. I want to go home and it's getting dark too." moaned Tanmay.

"Chill, we're almost there." said Robin.

"You've been saying that for the past one and half hour." replied Tanmay.

"Chill man, tomorrow is Sunday. It's not like we have office tomorrow. So let's go home late. For now lets' just explore the wilderness." convinced Robin.

"What the hell…." screamed Arun.

"What happened?" asked Robin.

The car started jerking and Arun stopped his car by the side of the road.

"My car is fucked. We need to find a garage." said Arun who has no idea what happened to his car.

The trio got down from the car.

"I guess this is the end of the adventure then?" said Tanmay who badly wanted to head home.

"Oh wait, what is that…." uttered Robin pointing towards a bright direction.

Everyone looks at the direction where Robin was pointing and noticed something amazing. A man who looked almost like a demy-god with a groovy turban, pointed mustache and a flamboyant costume was standing on the other side of the road with a camel that was dressed just like him. The camel looked stunning and flawless and to some extent delicious.

They all knew deep inside their minds that they had to approach this man. And they did.

As soon as they approached the man he started to sing. The boys were a bit confused but they didn't care much because he had a good voice. A god-like voice. After he sang for a good 30 seconds he put forward his right palm. The boys looked in their pockets for change. Arun takes out a 20 rupee note and gives it to the man.

"Thank you saab. Usually people give me coins but you gave me a note. God bless you boys." said the marwadi and then turned around to go away.

"Wait!" murmured Arun, "How much for the camel?"

"What?" replied the marwadi who was confused.

"How much for that good looking camel?" asked Arun again with a louder tone.

"It's not for sale."

"Why not?"

"From where we come, we don't sell our family members."

"Oh, I understand." said Arun who then looked at Robin and Tanmay.

They quickly removed out their wallets and gave their money to Arun. Arun removed his own wallet and took out the cash.

While Arun was busy counting the cash Robin and Tanmay rushed to the nearest ATM to get more cash. And after they handed the cash to Arun he firmly said, "Will 20000 rupees be enough for your camel?"

The marwadi man reached out to the camel's neck, took out the rope that is tied to its neck, hands the rope to Arun, took the money and walked away swiftly.

Our boys were just standing there. It was dark now. With no money left, the boys had to venture in an unknown dimension with only a magical camel and a car that doesn't work in their possession.

"What do we do now?" whispered Tanmay.

"Now we finish the job. We're going to kill this camel and we're going to eat this camel." replied Arun.

"Are you sure?" questioned Tanmay.

"Yes, he's right Tanmay. We have put too much effort to just leave now. Let's finish our mission." said Robin.

"Um, guys… Do you realize how high we are right now." asked Tanmay.

"Very fucking high! High as the last cloud in the fucking sky!" screamed Robin.

"Yes exactly. Since we're very high don't you think we're making a huge fucked up mistake? Don't you think we should just go home now?" cried Tanmay.

"Yes, you're right. We are making a huge mistake. But let's finish this mistake because there's nothing more sad than an incomplete mistake." replied Robin.

"Yes, he's right. Let's not leave this mistake unattended." echoed Arun.

"So what do you have in mind?" asked Tanmay.

"Simple, we're going to kill this camel and we're going to eat this camel." replied Arun.

"Except there's one problem." said Tanmay.

"And what's that?" asked Arun.

"How the fuck are we going to do it?" asked Tanmay.

"We'll figure it out. Don't worry." convinced Arun.

"I think we should go buy some knives." said Robin.

"What? Why in the world should we buy knives now? Haven't we spent enough money?" yelled Tanmay.

"You idiot. How the fuck are we supposed to kill this camel without knives. Let's buy some knives, cut it down and then figure a way to cook it." replied Robin.

And so the boys ventured into their new endeavor to get some weapons to complete the task at hand. But there was a problem. They had a camel and they had to take it with them. The boys tried pulling the camel's leash but it would barely move. With great difficulty they made the camel move two steps. Finally they gave up.

"Hey listen, Tanmay. Arun and I will go to that supermarket over there and buy some knives and stuff. You just stay put and guard the camel." ordered Robin.

"But why me?" asked Tanmay.

"Just do it man. We'll be right back." ensured Robin.

While Tanmay was standing there guarding the camel, Robin and Arun went to the supermarket to find some knives with barely any money in their pockets.

The supermarket had a wide variety of knives and they didn't know which one to buy. They ended up buying six knives, small, big, thin, large, they had it all.

"Oh shit. I just realized man." said Robin.

"Realized what?" asked Arun.

"We're about to sober down."

"So? So what?"

"We're doing a huge mistake and when we sober down we'll realize what a huge fucked up mistake we had just committed."

"Oh shit."

"There's only one solution."

"What?"

"Since we're in the supermarket we might as well buy some booze. That'll stop us from sobering down."

"You're right. Let's not sober down. Let's not leave this mistake undone."

They ended up standing in front of the cashier smelling like stale whisky. They could barely stand still and everyone in the supermarket noticed how drunk they were.

While they were getting the billing done for their booze and knives a police officer who was standing behind them started looking at them very suspiciously.

"What's with all the knives?" he asked.

To which Robin replied, "Oh these are for cooking, sir."

"Why would you drunk boys need so many knives, it looks to me like you boys are heading for a riot." said the officer in a slow tone.

"Hahahaha, no sir. We're good boys. These are for cooking and cutting meat." said Arun.

"Okay fine, you may go now. But you boys better not go driving." said the officer.

The boys paid the bill with whatever little money they had and swiftly got out of the supermarket.

"Oh boy. Hope we never meet that man again." says Robin wiping his forehead.

"You're damn right…. wait, wait, wait, wait. Where the fuck is our camel?" yelled Arun.

"Oh my god! I don't see it either and where's Tanmay?" asked Robin.

Clueless enough not knowing what to do next they both run to the spot where Arun's car was parked only to find Tanmay passed out in the back seat.

Robin starts shaking Tanmay's shoulder in an attempt to wake him up.

"Wake up you pig." yelled Robin.

When Robin turned around he saw Arun leaning towards the gutter and puking the life out of him.

"Dude Arun, don't pass out now man. We just bought fresh booze." said Robin.

"Fuck off man. This is all your fault. You wanted camel meat right? See where we are right now."

"So do I have to finish the new bottle all by myself?"

"Do what you want you bastard. Let me just puke and pass out in peace."

Arun opens the front door and passes out in the driver's seat.

Robin found a cigarette in Tanmay's pocket which he pulled out and began to smoke.

Five minutes later he passed out.

They woke up the next morning one by one. Arun was the first one to wake up and Tanmay the last.

"What the fuck! What the fuck! Why? Why? Why god why?" cried Arun at the top of his voice.

"Calm down man." whispered Robin rubbing his eyes and still recovering from the hangover.

"Calm down?" asked Arun in a loud voice.

"Dude, I'm having a terrible hangover right now. You don't have to shout man." replied Robin.

"Calm down? Do you remember anything about the camel?" asked Arun.

"Holy fuck. The camel." exclaimed Robin.

"I think I'm going to kill myself. I blew up my entire year's savings last night." cried Tanmay.

"What do we do now?" asked Robin.

"I don't know, you tell us. We're in this mess because of you anyways." replied Arun.

"I don't know. Let me think." said Robin.

After a while of silence their minds became numb. Not knowing what to say, Robin whispered, "What if, what if we go back to the same place where we met the marwadi hippy? Maybe we can find him there?"

"Since we don't have a better idea right now, I think we should do that." says Arun.

The boys walked to the same spot where they found the marwadi but they couldn't find him.

But Robin wasn't disheartened. Instead a glimpse of smile could be found upon his face.

"Why are you even smiling?" asked Tanmay, "We lost all our money and now we can't even find that camel man."

"Yes, but look up." said Robin pointing towards a white cloud on an otherwise empty sky.

"What's up there?" asked Arun.

"A cloud." replied Robin.

"I can see that but before I decide to murder you, can you please explain why you're doing what you're doing. Because I thought we're here looking for something else." screamed Arun.

Robin began to walk swiftly towards the direction of the cloud.

"Robin, Robin." shouted Tanmay and Arun in unison but that didn't stop him.

With no other option the boys began to follow Robin.

"Hey Robin, why are we even walking here? This place smells of garbage." screamed Tanmay.

Unaffected, Robin continued walking.

"The cloud never fails. It'll lead me to my destiny." whispered Robin.

"What is wrong with you? That's it we're going back." yelled Arun.

"Wait boys, look there." whispered Robin pointing under the cloud.

"What's there? I can only see a pile of garbage." replied Tanmay.

"But what do you see in that corner, at the end of the road?" asked Robin.

"A camel. Oh my God! Our camel and the marwadi hippy." exclaimed Arun.

"How did he get the camel back? Did he steal it from us?" asked Tanmay.

"Who cares? Let's go get our money back." ordered Arun.

The very next moment the boys began to run towards the marwadi.

As soon as the marwadi saw these three boys on his vision's horizon running towards him he sensed trouble. He abandoned his camel, turned around and ran. Behind him was a huge garbage dumping area and the marwadi ran right into it.

The boys hesitated to chase him through the garbage.

"Are you sure we should chase him now?" asked Tanmay who was hygiene conscious.

"We are stinking anyways. What difference does it make?" said Robin.

"Without our money, we may have to live in the garbage. So we might as well catch that bastard." yelled Arun.

"Are you sure Arun?" whispered Tanmay.

"Oh Tanmay, if I was Moses I would have split the garbage to make way. But you know we have no choice. Now let's run fuckers!" ordered Arun who then led the boys into the garbage chase.

They were running on two feet of garbage. Booze bottles, animal excrement, used condoms, blood; they were all stepped on.

They were running their fastest but the marwadi hippy eventually outran them. They lost sight of him but they didn't lose hope. They kept running.

Suddenly Tanmay tripped and fell. The other boys stopped to help him get on his feet.

"Be careful man." said Robin as he helped Tanmay get on his feet.

"How did you fall?" asked Arun.

"I don't know. I just stepped on that and tripped." answered Tanmay pointing towards an object in the garbage.

Robin stared at that peculiar object for a while, took a deep breath, and gathered enough air in his lungs to say, "Jesus, what is that? Is that a bloody head?"

PART FOURTEEN

THE DAY

There will be a day in everyone's life that will make their lives different forever. Not just any day but 'the day'. The day that will cause a life changing effect. The day that will make all the other days feel shorter. This was the first day of the rest of their lives.

Today was that day for Robin, Arun and Tanmay.

The Frazer Town Police Station was awfully noisy that day thanks to these boys.

"What's the matter? Why are you all shouting at the same time? Can you boys calm down?" shouted the police officer seated on a wooden chair with his fat ponch dropping out of his belt.

"A head, a bloody head. That's what we saw. We saw a head." screamed Robin.

"A head? Head of what? Head of which organization?" asked the officer.

"Not that head. The head. The other head. A human head." replied Robin.

"Wait, wait, calm down. Now tell me slowly what happened? asked the officer.

The boys told them the entire story behind finding the head. Everything from drinking to marwadi hippy to camel to finding a beheaded head in the garbage.

"And what else? That's it?" asked the officer once the boys were done illustrating the whole head finding episode.

"What do you mean by 'That's it' officer?" asked Arun.

"You boys seriously expect me to believe this? How much did you boys drink? Are you boys on drugs right now? Do you know how much work we have? We have to deal with robbers and murderers and rapists everyday and to make our work more difficult we have kids like you coming here to pester us inside out. Get out of here right now or I'll have to lock you up in the cage." shouted the officer who was extremely frustrated after listening to the boys' tale.

"I knew you wouldn't believe us officer. But then again who would? Which is why I clicked a picture of the head." replied Arun who then picks out his cellphone and shows the officer the picture of the head.

"Okay, this better be real. I'm still very skeptical of this but I'm going to send two cops to the spot right now.

We're going to have to identify the victim. I'm scared to ask but do you boys by any chance know who the victim is?" asked the officer curiously.

"Yes. His name was Alan. He was our friend." replied Robin.

"So you boys were chasing some camel man in the middle of a dump yard because he stole your money which you gave it to him in the first place and while chasing him someone slipped and you found a dead head of one your friend. That's what you're trying to tell me right?" asked the officer.

"Yes sir. That is correct." replied Arun.

"If what you're saying is the truth, then I guess this will be the simplest case I've ever worked on." said the officer.

"What? Really? How?" asked Robin.

"Because then I would have to assume you were the murderers and arrest you." replied the officer.

"Look I know this sounds bizarre and unusual but we didn't kill him and everything we've said was the truth." said Robin.

"Regardless of whether you've killed him or not you boys are hereby obligated to accompany us to that spot." ordered the officer.

"Gladly." replied Arun.

And so the boys and the cops went to the spot. But by the time they reached there the news of the gutter head had spread like wild fire and there was a big crowd and two local news trucks by the spot to cover the incident.

"Ah! The journalists! Always on time and always before us." exclaimed the officer.

"Well, what do we do now officer?" asked Robin.

"Now we're going to take that head for an examination, hopefully we find the rest of the body. Also we're going to need your fingerprints among other things and we'll ask you a few questions. Don't worry, we'll catch the culprits." replied the officer.

"Oh man, this has been the worst day of my life. We better call Alan's parents and inform them." said Tanmay.

"You don't have to do that, they'll come to know anyways." said the officer.

"What? How?" asked Tanmay.

"There are two news trucks here already. By the end of the day everybody's parents will know what happened here." replied the officer.

"Okay, so can we go home now?" asked Tanmay.

"For now, ya. You can go home. But don't leave town." replied the officer.

The tired boys then called a cab and headed back to their respective homes to spend the rest of their beautiful Sunday evening.

PART FIFTEEN

RESURRECTION

"No, not you again." screamed Robin.

"Yes, yes it's me." replied his father.

"I'm tired of you invading my dreams."

"Look at you. You're in dire straits. You're dreams need invasion. It needs to be invaded by someone who can straighten you up."

"What are you here for now? Are you going to give me another lecture?"

"Maybe…. anyways I'm here to talk to you about your cloud."

"Oh, not the cloud again. Last time I followed that stupid cloud of yours I ended up finding a head. A dead head."

"Stupid cloud of mine? It's not mine, it's yours."

"My what? My punishment."

"No, not your punishment. Your escape."

"Escape from what? Sanity?"

"No, escape from life. An escape from your day to day, mundane, ordinary, boring life. Isn't that the point after all?"

"Point after all? What point?"

"The point of escape. The point of resurrection."

"Resurrection? Who's resurrection?"

"Yours"

"Mine? But I don't need to be resurrected. I'm not dead to be resurrected."

"Every man has dead child buried under his soul which needs to be resurrected."

"What? What are you talking about? Man, what are you tripping on?"

"You know exactly what I'm talking about. Look at yourself. You twenty something under-achieved piece of shit. You confused yet healthy young adult who's submerged in a quarter life crisis."

"Stop describing me and just come to the point."

"Remember how optimistic you were when you were younger?"

"Ya, I remember. My optimism back then was a result of my ignorance about the world. Now that I know how the world works I've become less optimistic for important reasons such as ummm…. survival."

"Oh bullshit. What? You're gonna blame the world now for your problems?"

"All my problems exist because of the way this world is. So obviously I'll blame the world."

"All your problems exist because you exist. So the only person you should be blaming is yourself. And besides stop pushing your problems to the world, it has enough problems already."

"What do I do then?"

"You've got no choice but to follow the cloud. It's your only escape. You need that cloud. Without it your life is just stale. You need to start living your life because what you're doing right now is just a mere imitation of life"

"Why are you telling me all this?"

"I'm not. You are."

"What?"

"At the end of the day I'm a product of your memory, a figment of your imagination. I can only tell you what you've always longed to hear."

Robin woke up.

PART SIXTEEN

THE FIRST DAY
OF THE REST OF OUR LIVES

The boys were at the bar again. This time they were drinking light beer as they were well aware of what happened the last time they got hammered.

"Hey, I heard you quit your job Robin." asked Tanmay.

"Yup, you heard right." replied Robin.

"How come?" asked Arun.

"Man, where do I start? It was bad enough that the job was frustrating by itself but then it got worse after all my colleagues saw our faces on the news channels after Alan's murder. Everyone in my office thinks I'm some kind of a murderer. They're all so paranoid about me.

I could hear people murmuring about me and people would always stare at me whenever I went to hit the loo. I couldn't even take a shit in peace." explained Robin.

"Well, same here bro." said Arun.

"I hope this case is solved soon. But until then everyone we'll think we did it." said Tanmay.

"Who do you think might have done it?" asked Robin.

"I've got no clue. What kind of a person would want to kill Alan. He couldn't even hurt a fly if he wanted to." replied Arun.

"So Robin, what are you going to do now that you're unemployed?" asked Tanmay.

"I guess I'll just lay low for a while. Just chill for a few months." replied Robin.

"Are you planning to go to your hometown?" asked Tanmay.

"No way man. What'll I do there? And besides, if I leave this town more people will think I'm the killer and have gone absconding. And the last thing I want to do right now is meet my mother." replied Robin.

"So you're absconding from your mom, ah?" asked Tanmay.

"Hahaha, exactly." replied Robin.

"So does she know about the murder?" asked Arun.

"Of course she does. This thing was all over TV. And ever since she saw me on TV she's asking me to come back." replied Robin.

"We're all screwed from all angles, aren't we?" asked Arun.

"Ya, you're right. Our lives are changed forever. This is the first day of the rest of the rest of our lives." replied Robin.

"All right guys. I guess it's time to go now." concluded Tanmay.

The boys paid the bill and headed back home.

Robin decided to walk home as his house was close by. Suddenly his phone started ringing. It was an unknown number. He picked the call and said, "Hello?"

"It's me."

"Asha?"

"Can we meet?"

"Where have you been."

"It's a long story. Listen can we meet?"

"Ya sure. But why the urgency?"

"Everything is so fucked up. We need to meet right now!"

"Okay, okay. Where do you want to meet?"

"Somewhere secluded."

PART SEVENTEEN

CONTAINER

Robin decided to meet Asha in a parking lot of an old building as per her advice.

"I missed you so much Robin." said Asha.

"Then why did you leave me? Why did you stop responding to my calls?"

"For safety."

"Safety? Who's safety?"

"Yours…. and mine."

"Safety from what? Safety from whom?"

"Haven't you been watching the news lately? Some guy's head got chopped off."

"Watching the news? I've been living that news. That guy who's head got chopped off was my friend and some people think I chopped his head. You've got to believe me, I didn't chop off his head."

"Of course you didn't. But I know who did it. I know who chopped off Alan's head."

"What? How do you know who chopped off his head? Do you know Alan?"

"Yes I do."

"How do you know Alan?"

"How do you think I know Alan?"

"Wait what? Oh God! You know, I'm not even that surprised. Alan did seem like a guy who would one day lose his virginity to a prostitute."

"Well....... so did you! I guess that's a quality that you and Alan share together."

"Oh Jesus Christ! Just kill me now. Wish it had been my head that was chopped and thrown in the dumpyard. So you're telling me that Alan fucked you right?"

"Yes. I don't know how he got my number but he got it and he called me. And he fucked me. If I knew he was your friend I would've probably avoided that. And he's not the only person I had sex with for money. There's a long line of men. I'm a prostitute. This is what I do. I thought you already knew that."

"Ya, you're right. I'm sorry. But how do you know who killed him? Who killed him?"

"It was Rajan."

"Rajan? Rajan who?"

"Rajan, the rowdy. The gangster who has half the politicians in his pocket."

"Oh my God. Wait a minute, I think I know who you're talking about. Rajan, that… that old rich guy who's famous for doing things that are illegal. He owns things and he comes on the TV from time to time because he's got many politician friends, wait, are we talking about the same guy."

"Yes we are."

"Why would he kill someone like Alan?"

"He didn't kill Alan. He ordered his men to kill Alan."

"Okay. But why would he want Alan dead?"

"Because he thought Alan was you."

"What? You mean to say that he wanted me dead?"

"Yes, he wanted you dead."

"Why would he want someone like me dead? Was it also because he thought I was someone else?"

"I wish I could say that, but he really wanted you dead."

"But why?"

"Because people like you meant bad business to him?"

"What? How is that even possible?"

"Rajan runs a lot of illegal businesses. Drugs, money laundering, racketeering, prostitution and so on. And prostitution gets him big money. If anybody falls in love with his hookers and distracts them then he'll get rid of them. As far as I know he has killed a few men in the past few years for 'distracting' his girls. Now do you know how you fit his target." explained Asha.

"Uh…"

"I'm sorry you're in trouble because of me."

"No, it's not your fault. Don't blame yourself."

"We need get out of this city soon."

"Why?"

"Because when Rajan finds out he was supposed to kill you instead of your friend, it'll be too late for you."

"We better report this to the police."

"Hahaha, what? Are you nuts? Listen to yourself?"

"Ya, you're right. That was a bad idea."

"Let's just catch a bus, train, whatever and get out of here before someone finds us."

"I can't."

"What? Why not?"

"I don't want to go. I can't imagine hiding for the rest of my life."

"Why not?"

"Because that's what I've been doing all my life. And I'm through that. Been there, done that. Enough's enough. I'm not running anywhere."

"Hiding all your life? I'm the one who's supposed to say that."

"Alright fine. You win. You've been hiding all your life and now I'm supposed to decide whether I want to hide with someone who's been hiding all her life. Well, no"

"Would you rather get killed?"

"Oh Asha! Why run? Run away to where? Run away from who? Run away from some guy who we think might kill us? I don't know what to do. But I really don't want to run away with someone who's name I don't even know. I mean, I don't even know who you are. When I was calling you all these days you never cared to pick up or call me back. And now you come here all of a sudden and want me to run away with you, just like that. I mean, I mean what were you even thinking? What was the plan, who are you? Do you even have a real name? I'm really not sure about…."

"Ruchita, it's Ruchita. Now that you know my name can we run away?"

"Wait, what? Like, this is getting really confusing. People usually want to know a hundred things before going on a simple date and you tell me one thing and you want me to elope with you. How can I even trust you? How do I know you're not actually secretly working for Rajan and you want me dead?"

"If that was the case you'd be dead already. Listen, I'm not forcing you to run away with me. I'm going to leave this town soon anyways and I thought you'd want to come too considering the circumstances."

"What's the worst that could happen?"

"Death"

"Okay, that's pretty bad. Listen why don't you come over to my place so we can discuss more about this?"

"No fucking way. The police and the journalists already know where you're living. Right now I'm living in a cheap hotel that's almost untraceable. If I come over to your place that'll make things a lot worse. Rajan may find out and he may well, you know, separate our heads from our bodies."

"Okay fine. Say, I decide to leave town with you, then what, where do we go?"

"Anywhere. Preferably out of this state. We could live in a small beach town in Goa or in the hills of Manali. We could start a small shop and sell stuff at overpriced rates to white tourists. I guess that would be nice."

"What? I mean what? Like do you even think about what you're saying? Like who are you? Seriously Asha, sorry Ruchita or whatever your name is, who are you?" asked Robin.

"I don't know. I've been trying to figure that out my whole life. But I was never really given a chance. Maybe now after I run away I'll have enough time to figure out who I am. I don't really know who my parents are. They say I was born somewhere in Maharashtra. I can barely remember anything about my childhood. It's all so blurry and dull. I just remember living as a kid in some dark place with dim red lights, then when I was 12 I guess, I think I got sold or something and I was brought down to the state border area where for the first time some strange man…"

Robin could see her eyes tearing up. He tried his best to hold back his own tears but eventually gave up.

"Now do you realize why I just want to run away and get lost? I don't mind running away alone. But I've been alone all my life. And for the first time I found someone who for some weird reason likes me a little. And I just thought 'Hey, maybe I should have an adventure, an escape with someone who likes me', someone who I could call a friend. Look I didn't want to get too close to you at first because I didn't want to put your life in danger. But now, hahaha, fuck it. Everything is so screwed. Let's just run for it. Are you in?" asked Asha.

"Oh! Ummm…. Uff. Fuck, wait, let me think, let me think. Well, this is just going way over my head. Can I get some time and let you know because running away isn't exactly a decision that one could make in an hour."

"Ya, sure. I'll be leaving town coming Saturday at 4 in the evening. I'll just go to the station and catch a random train that goes anywhere far. You don't even have to tell me you're coming. All you have to do is show up on time."

"Wait, are you leaving on Saturday? What day is today?"

"Today's Thursday."

"Thursday, Friday, satur… Oh wait I've got to decide in two days."

"That's right. You've got two days. I hope that's enough to make up your mind. I'll be waiting for you at the station. See ya."

Ruchita kisses him goodbye and leaves the spot.

PART EIGHTEEN

TO KNOW THAT IT'S BEST NOT TO KNOW

Robin was lying on the bed contemplating the ceiling fan go round and round and round. He tried to sleep but the voice in his head kept bothering him with too many questions. He somehow managed to suppress the voices and dozed off his way to sleep. He woke up a minute later and noticed a familiar old man sitting on the chair next to his bed.

"Oh, thank God you're here." exclaimed Robin.

"You cried for help, how can I not show up?"

"Okay, what do I do now?"

"Why are you asking me? It's your decision to make, not mine."

"What? You're partially responsible for the situation I'm in right now and you have nothing to say. All these times when I never asked for any advice you would shove your loud mouth into my dreams and now when I'm desperately in need for your guidance you have nothing to say. C'mon dad, say something. Enlighten me."

"Well, son, I can only tell you what you want to listen, what you already know. At the end of the day I'm just a figment of your imagination."

"Oh, shut up. Shut the fuck up. We both know you're not just a mere figment of my mind. You're more than that. You're an asshole with a deep voice who can convince me to do things I couldn't convince myself. C'mon now, say something, say anything. If you could convince me to follow some stupid cloud, some stupid fucking stoned cloud, then I bet you could convince me to do anything. Say something man. Should I leave town?"

"I'm afraid I don't have all the answers. It's better at many instances not to know anything. Better to be a happy fool than a suicidal genius."

"What? What are you talking about? It's good to be smart right? It's good to have a lot of answers."

"Not necessarily. Look at all the people around you. You're surrounded by clueless people who don't know anything and yet they are so happy. But look at all those psychologists. The good psychologists, they know so much about the human behavior that I can only imagine how depressed they must be all the time. They know so much about life that they must have realized by now how pointless it is to live life and they must have contemplated suicide at least a couple of times. Every psychologist is at the risk of becoming a psycho. It's ironic that these psychos are hired to treat the 'socially deemed psychos'. So son, the best advice I can give you is to know nothing. At least the curiosity will keep you alive. Stay dumb, stay alive. Don't try to know everything about life. Don't try to be a psychologist, you'll end up being depressed."

"But dad, weren't you teaching psychology at college?"

"Yes I did. Why do you think I killed myself?"

PART NINETEEN

TIME FOR THE WAVE
TO BREAK AND ROLL BACK

The police were extremely frustrated. Inspector Arvind was appointed to investigate the case of 'the garbage head'. The officer who was working at the local police station who was appointed to assist Inspector Arvind was Inspector Hari.

Right outside the police station stood a small kiosk where the cops were regular customers. Arvind and Hari went there to fetch a cup of chai. While Inspector Hari smoked a small, Inspector Arvind lit his kings.

"I don't know what we can do about this." utters Inspector Arvind.

"Yeah, this case looks like a dead end. If we don't close this case very soon the media will eat us up." says Inspector Hari.

"What do you guys usually do during such cases?"

"Well you know, we just catch hold of a rowdy, we lock him up, we strip him and we beat him till he admits that he's done the murder."

"That's it? Is it that simple?"

"No it can get complicated sometimes. We may have to bribe the rowdy, we may have to get a lawyer to represent that rowdy, bribe the lawyer. We may also have to talk to a few journalists, plant some evidence and make the media say what we want them to. There's quite a lot of work involved."

"But it works, right?"

"Yeah definitely, in most cases. When we're struggling to close a long pending case we adopt such methods. It's got a good success rate."

"Oh good. But from where do you get the money to pay the bribe to all those parties."

"We pay bribe from the bribe we make."

"Okay, so you're telling me that you guys end up paying bribe from the bribe that you guys collect from other activities right. Does that work out, like financially?"

"Yeah, yeah. We always end up with a bribe surplus."

"Oh great! So if we are unable to close this case by next month can we do the same for this case as well?"

"Ooh. I don't think so. This is a very high profile case. The media is covering this case from 360 degrees. Our superiors are asking updates regularly. And there are rumors that one of Rajan's men maybe behind this. With superiors, politicians, big shots and journalists following our every step it maybe next to impossible for us to fake a murderer."

"Hmmm, okay Hari. Let's go back inside the station. Let's see what we can do."

And so the two police officers headed back to the station after a very fruitful conversation.

There was a huge noisy racket taking place around the station. All the cops were running around shouting and questioning.

Inspector Arvind and Inspector Hari were confused.

"What's happening here? What's all the noise for?" asks Inspector Arvind.

"Look at that." yells a constable pointing at a person who sat by the entrance of the station.

What the Inspectors saw that day shocked their very souls into a frozen state.

They saw a tired man, covered in blood. With blood stains all over his shirt, stab marks around his ankle, black mud sticking on his forehead he looked like a post apocalyptic black metal zombie.

"Just when we thought things couldn't get any worse." whispered Inspector Hari.

Inspector Arvind walked straight towards the man and stards at his devilish face for two long minutes.

"Oh wait. Wait a minute. You have a familiar face. I think I've seen you before. What's your name sir?" asked Inspector Arvind.

The man lifts his tired face slowly but surely with great difficulty and he utters his name out of his mouth, "Robin"

PART TWENTY

DEMENTED, YET SPIRITUAL?
(THE DAY BEFORE)

The day had come for Robin to decide. To stay or to flee. A flying bird he could be. Nevertheless trapped. Trapped in the cage of his own mind. Trapped with questions. Questions with no answers. Answers which if he did find would lead him to more questions. An unknown future. A dark past. Stuck in between was our Robin. With these words echoing within the walls of his skull and the valleys of his mind, he was tortured. Tortured with everything. With everyone. With every passing second. His mind was numb. The line between reality and insanity was now blurred. Hopeless, demented, hungry, confused and lost.

But he still had an important decision to make.

"Should I stay or should I run away with Ruchita?"

Meanwhile three kilometers away Ruchita was waiting in the railway station for a man who she hoped would change her life for the better and provide her an escape which she rightfully deserves.

"I hope he shows up." she said to herself. She had suffered enough. She was lonely her entire life. Born to an identity crisis. Now was her time to create a new identity. To give life a new purpose. And all she wanted was a man who she barely knew. A man who she believed was rightfully made for her.

She waited and waited. And the time had come to leave. She had two tickets in her hand which would take them to Goa. But it looked like she might only need one as the man who she hoped would show up was not in sight.

She could see the smoke coming out of the chimney of the train on the horizon. She turned around and looked everywhere desperately hoping he would show up but alas, he was still not to be seen.

The train had finally reached the platform and with no hope left to spare she hopped aboard the train.

The train brought back old memories to Ruchita. She was brought to the city by a train. A train was such a weird thing for her. A tube filled with people that moves itself along with the people in it. It goes through hills, mountains, valleys, jungles and slums. A person maybe lying on one spot on the universe. And the train can change that spot overnight.

"Huh, something tells me that I must've taken my first steps in a train." she said to herself.

She had a love-hate relationship with trains. Trains make her feel nostalgic. It brought back bittersweet memories.

"When was the last time I saw my parents? Was it on a train? Maybe I was snatched away from my parents on a train. I don't know. I wonder though, what else could have happened to me on a train that I might have forgotten that are now faded memories."

Ruchita talks to herself a lot. After all she was lonely her whole life. And this made her need company of others desperately.

"Oh I hate that Robin right now. That bastard. All he had to do was show up. I would have taken such good care of him. But now I've to sit here and talk to myself, maybe pretend he's here and talk to my version of Robin."

Suddenly a man wearing a grey monkey cap and a black sweater showed up and tapped Ruchita on the right shoulder with his finger.

"Ruchita, we need to get out of here." he whispered.

"What? Who are… wait? Robin? What are you doing here? I thought you wouldn't show up." she replied.

"Okay, Okay, but…"

Before he could say another word Ruchita gave him a tight hug and whispered into his ear, "I'm so glad you came. You've no idea how happy you just made me. It doesn't matter what the outcome of this is anymore because you're here. And that's all that matters to me."

"Okay, listen up. We need to get out here."

"Why? What happened?"

"We're being followed."

"Followed? Followed by whom?"

"I don't know. They maybe Rajan's men."

"That bloody Rajan. How did he find out?"

"I don't know. But we need to get out of here."

"Where are they right now?"

"They're in the next compartment."

"But Robin, how are you so sure it's them?"

"I just know, okay. I'll explain everything later, when the time is right. But first things first, we need to get out of this train."

"Okay."

Robin led Ruchita out of the train. With the hurry they were in, Ruchita forgot to take her bags along with her.

They got down in the next station which was in a small town by the outskirts of the city.

"Are they still following us? I think they must've lost sight of us by now." said Ruchita.

"Let's not underestimate them. Let's keep going." replied Robin.

Robin led Ruchita into the woods behind the station they got down from. They found a small lake where they stopped to gather their breath.

Gasping for breath Ruchita asked, "Are you sure you saw them? I didn't see them anywhere."

"Neither did I." replied Robin who then removed a small kitchen knife out of his socks.

"What? Robin what is this?" asked Ruchita.

Before she could say another word Robin stabbed her in the stomach.

"What? Why? Why? Why?" whispered Ruchita trying to comprehend the situation.

"I'm sorry. But this was the only way it had to end. I really liked you, I did. In fact I was in love with you. But look how complicated life got."

Ruchita who had fallen on the ground with a bleeding stomach cried out and said, "What? Please don't kill me. Save me…. please."

"I can't. You see, I need you to die. And besides it's too late now. Here's what I'm going to do. I'm going to stab you again. This time a little harder and then probably again until you stop breathing."

He looked down at Ruchita who spat out some blood as she screamed, "I wish I had never met you, you psycho. I don't deserve this. My life shouldn't be ending like this. I've suffered my whole life and this is how it ends. This is not fair. Please, I'm begging you. Don't do this. I want to live another day."

"I'm sorry. I know nothing is fair. You don't deserve to die but I deserve to kill you. Relax, dying isn't going to be even slightly as painful as the pain you've gone through all your life. I need to kill you. I have a problem. I want to go back to living my boring normal life. I can do that only if I kill you."

"You're going to complicate your life by killing me."

"No…. no, no, no, no, no, no, no. You don't get it. There's a reason for everything. Even for this. I hope I don't sound unreasonable, but I need you to die."

"You're demented, aren't you?"

"Yes, you're right. I'm demented, but also spiritual. Ever since I quit my job I had a lot of time in my hands. I started meditating, exercising and even reading. The other day I was reading the Gita and there was this one quote in the book which I memorized which goes, 'There never was a time when you or I did not exist. Nor will there be any future when we shall cease to be.' So relax Ruchita, you're not really going to die."

He then got on his knees and stabbed her again. He then threw the knife at her. With great difficulty Ruchita grabbed the knife and stabbed him twice on the leg. But they were not deep cuts as Ruchita didn't have enough energy to deliver deep stabs. Robin then kicked her wrist making the knife from her hand to go flying away.

"I'm sorry Ruchita. I really am. But killing you is my only escape back to normalcy. You don't deserve to die but I need you to. I love you Ruchita." he said looking into her beautiful dying eyes. He kissed her one last time and then he saw her breath her last.

He left her body lying there like a dead animal and he walked away.

He walked away with his lover's blood on his hands and hope in his mind. Hope that he can now return to normalcy.

PART TWENTY-ONE

RETURN TO NORMALCY/
NOSTALGIC PATH TO UTOPIA

Inspector Arvind and Inspector Hari brought Robin into the investigation room. They made him sit on a wooden chair. While inspector Hari was sitting facing Robin, Inspector Arvind preferred to stand.

"So tell us exactly what happened?" questioned Arvind.

Robin was shivering. Inspector Hari noticed this and asked if he wanted some water to which Robin replied in the affirmative. Inspector Hari obliged and got him some water.

"So are you feeling comfortable now?" asked Arvind.

Robin nodded his head.

"Okay so what happened?" asked Arvind.

"I killed a person." he replied.

"What?" screamed Arvind.

Both the officers were shocked to their nerves. There was silence in the room for a good two minutes.

Inspector Hari raised his forehead and asked, "Who did you kill?"

"I swear I didn't kill her on purpose. It was self defense." replied Robin.

"Okay, but who did you kill?" asked Arvind, "And tell us everything that led to the killing. And don't miss out a single detail, if you don't want to be thrown into a cell. Tell us everything."

"Okay here's what happened. During Alan's last days he would get drunk very often and he would start talking about some prostitute and the time he spent with her. I thought he was bluffing. He kept telling me that he would meet her every week to have sex with her. I didn't believe him because Alan wasn't capable of doing such a thing. He would tell me what kind of a slut she was and how he would use her and even beat her sometimes. He also told me that on certain occasions he wouldn't pay her. I didn't believe a word he said because I just couldn't imagine someone like Alan who had a good-boy image his entire life do such a thing. Plus he was drunk when he was talking. So I assumed it was the alcohol talking and not him. But then his murder happened. And then my whole perception of him changed. Nobody knew who the suspect was. But I thought I knew. Everything Alan told me about that prostitute came back to my mind." answered Robin who stopped abruptly to drink some more water.

"Okay, go on." demanded Inspector Hari.

"So like I said, everything he said about her came back to my mind. He told me she would take him to cheap hotels where they would do their business. And like I had said earlier Alan wouldn't pay her sometimes which is why she killed him. She was pissed off with him. She was tired of being treated the way Alan was treating her. So she killed him." said Robin who wanted to say more but was interrupted by Inspector Arvind.

"Wait, wait, wait, wait. Are you trying to say that some prostitute killed Alan because he didn't pay her?" asked Inspector Arvind.

Robin nodded his head and answered, "Yes."

"And you killed to her avenge your friend's life?" asked Inspector Hari.

"No, I had to kill her. It was self defense." replied Robin.

"Okay so forget about the part where you killed the prostitute. Let's talk about that later. But are you sure that the prostitute killed your friend Alan?" asked Inspector Arvind.

"Yes, I'm sure." he replied.

"Good, then will you be willing to tell that in a court and do you think you could convince the court that your friend Alan was killed by that prostitute?" asked Inspector Arvind

"Yes, I think so. I hope so." he replied.

"Okay, good." replied Inspector Arvind who took Inspector Hari with him as he walked out of the interrogation room.

Once they came out of the room Inspector Hari asked Inspector Arvind, "Okay so what do we do now?"

"Okay, listen. We'll solve this one murder at a time. I think we can close the case of Alan's murder. We just have to worry about the new murder. That's all." replied Inspector Arvind as he puts his arm around Inspector Hari's shoulder.

"But what if he's lying? What if this prostitute didn't kill Alan? Then what?" asked Hari.

"Who cares? We need to close the case of Alan's murder. Let's make it look like she killed him and close the case. Anyways she's a dead prostitute. You can blame anything on a dead prostitute. Nobody will come to defend her. She probably doesn't have any family or friends to defend her. And the media will buy this story with ease. Let's plant some evidence, bend the investigation process, do everything we can to make it look like she killed him. Once we're done convincing the world that Alan's prostitute killed him, we can close his murder case and start worrying about the new one. Did Robin kill her in self defense or did he kill her to avenge his friend's death? I don't know. Let's leave that to the court to decide. Either way it's a win-win for us because we're closing cases, important cases that too. So step one, convince the world that an angry prostitute killed and beheaded her lonely customer, Alan. Are you with me?" concluded Inspector Arvind.

They stood there and spoke for a while in hush tones, laughed a little and then they headed back into the investigation room where Robin was still seated for some more questioning.

"Okay Robin, thank you for giving us a good amount of information and we hope the information that you've given us is reliable. However there are two murders in the scene right now. Wait…. any idea what the name of that prostitute is?" asked Inspector Arvind.

"Her name was Asha. But I'm not sure whether that's her real name. But Alan was calling her Asha." replied Robin.

"Okay. We'll try to find out who she is. But like I said there are two murders involved here. Asha killed Alan and you killed Asha. Fine, you know what? Fine. We're convinced that Asha killed Alan. Let's close that chapter. But you killed Asha and you said that it was in self defense. I didn't get that part. Could you explain exactly how that happened?" questioned Inspector Arvind.

"Well…. well, where do I start? Okay, here goes. I thought that Alan's hooker had killed him because of the way he was treating her. And this thought of mine wanted me to find her. But it was very difficult to find her. I tried finding her on the internet. No luck there. If you type 'prostitutes in Bangalore' half of those girls' names will turn out to be Asha or some other similar name. But then I remembered, Alan used to get drunk and say completely random things like, he used to say that he would go to a railway station on the outskirts of the city which was painted all red. And he said on that red platform he could score all the drugs he wanted. And one thing I clearly remember him saying was that he could get the best pussy on this red platform. So I did some research on railway stations and then decided to go to Yeshwanthpur railway station. This station was huge but according to Alan's description of the red railway station where he went, one would think it's a small station with a single platform. And besides this station wasn't exactly on the outskirts. So I caught a train there and travelled to Nelamangala which was on the outskirts and as I looked out the window I suddenly saw a small station which was painted reddish brown and I decided to get down there." explained Robin.

"Okay you got down there, fine. Then what? What happened when you got there?" asked Inspector Hari.

"Hmmm… That station had a very dark vibe. It was almost deserted. But there were a few people there. Strange people. Kids selling toys, beggars and even peddlers. Some guy just walked close to me and asked whether I wanted some hashish. I just looked the other way and walked away. But to make things worse, some transgender people, you know, those hijdas, they approached me. They even invited me for sex. I declined and walked away. But then I wanted to find this prostitute badly. And I didn't have a clue how to find her. I had travelled so far and I didn't want to return without finding this girl. So in a desperate attempt I walked back to those hijdas who were thrilled to see me again. I told them that I wanted a prostitute, a female prostitute, a fully female prostitute. Disgusted by my demand they walked away abusing me. But one of them came back and demanded a hundred rupees. I gave it to her and she told me where I could find female prostitutes. So I followed the directions that were provided to me by that hijda. I walked by the tracks. I walked for one kilometer, maybe two. And I found a lodge. It was painted yellow but it looked brown because it was old." explained Robin who then demanded a break.

The inspectors obliged. They got some tea and cigarettes into the investigation room. They all sipped their chais and smoked their cigarettes. They spoke some non murder related stuff for about fifteen minutes. Robin cracked a few jokes and made the inspectors laugh. The inspectors were glad to see the humorous side of Robin. They were also glad that he was now more comfortable talking to them.

"Yes, you were saying that you saw some old hotel, some lodge around one or two kilometers from the railway station. Does that place have a name?" asked Inspector Arvind.

"Ya, ya, it has a name. I saw an old rusted board right on top of the entrance which had its name 'Karuna' written on it." replied Robin.

"Oh that place. That place is quite famous in our books." said Inspector Hari, "Famous for all the wrong reasons."

"Really? Famous for what?" asked Inspector Arvind.

"Drugs, prostitution, those kinds of things are what makes that place famous in our books." answered Inspector Hari.

"Excuse us for a few minutes." said Inspector Arvind who then took Inspector Hari out of the room.

"Okay, send some of our men there right now and start the investigation. Search every inch of that lodge, every spot around that place and find everything you can." ordered Inspector Arvind to which Inspector Hari obliged.

Inspector Hari called the Nelamangala police station and made arrangements for the investigation. The police officers along with their constables and the police dogs rushed to the spot and found a dead body by the lake a few hundred meters away from Karuna lodge.

Meanwhile Robin is alone with Inspector Arvind.

"So tell me boy, what happened once you reached the lodge?"

"That lodge was a very dark place. But I thought I would find her there. So I went in. All the windows in that place were locked. All the lights were dim. As soon as I entered a man approached me and asked what I was doing there. And I told him I'm looking for Asha. He told me to go outside the lodge from the back door and wait there. So I did. I waited and after a while out came a girl. That girl was beautiful. I mean…. she was beautiful. Just beautiful. The most beautiful thing that I've ever seen. Then I thought to myself, it's a pity that someone so beautiful has ended up in such a filthy place. She told me that her fee was three thousand rupees. I said okay. She also told me that the rooms were full which made me wonder where would we be making love. She giggled and whispered into my ear, 'Come with me, there's an empty lake close by'. So I thought great, we'll have sex by the lake."

"Wait, wait, hold on. Sorry for interrupting but are you telling me the truth or are you narrating me every man's sexual fantasy?"

"It's the truth."

"What the hell. Why can't such things happen to me? Anyways, for your sake I hope this story ends well. Go on, tell me what happened after you reached the lake although I think I know what's going to happen?"

"Okay, we went by the lake. I was just looking around to make sure nobody was watching us. She laughed and said, 'Relax nobody is watching us' and then she just casually asked, 'How did you know my name, who told you about me, was it one of my other customers?'"

"Okay, so what did you say?"

"I told her that I had heard about her from a friend of mine called Alan. When I said the word 'Alan' I saw a sudden change of expression on her face."

"And that's when you decided to kill her?"

"No, no, no, I killed her in self defense. Wait, let me complete."

"Okay fine, complete."

"Then she asked me, 'which Alan? I know a lot of Alans.' to which I replied, 'You know. The Alan who's dead. The Alan who's head was cut off. The Alan who's head was thrown in the garbage. The Alan who would fuck you and not pay you.'"

"Were you talking with this prostitute in English or Kannada?"

"English"

"Was her English good English or bad English?"

"Good English"

"So are you telling me that you went to a terrible looking hotel in a cheap area where you found a woman who looks like an angel who also speaks fluent English. What are the odds of that?"

"What? You don't believe me?"

"No, I believe you but what are the odds, eh? Anyways, you continue. Tell me what happened then?"

"Then she started to panic. She started walking away from me. I started yelling, 'come back here'. She didn't respond. So I caught her arm. She turned around and punched my nose. I started yelling even more. I yelled out, 'You killed Alan didn't you?' and she asked me to fuck off. I caught her in the arm tightly and told her, 'I'm not letting you go anywhere until you tell me everything'. Suddenly she removed out a knife. As soon as I saw the knife I punched her. I knocked her to the ground."

"You punched a girl?"

"What else was I supposed to do? It was self defense. I swear. Anyways, that happened and then I thought she was unconscious. So I went close to her and she stabbed my ankle. Twice!"

Robin showed Inspector Arvind the cuts on his ankle.

"Shit! Those cuts look quite deep. I think you may need some medical attention."

"That's okay, anyways, where was I? Right, yeah like I said, she stabbed me on my ankle, so I kicked her wrist and the knife went flying. I ran to grab the knife. She jumped on me from the back and started strangling my neck with her arms. And damn man, she was one strong girl. I just pulled her and tossed her on the ground and went for the knife. When I turned around she started punching and slapping me. She tried to pull the knife from my hand. And that's when…."

"That's when what?"

"That's when I stabbed her. I stabbed her once. And she started screaming. I thought she would call some men from the lodge who would then come and kill me. So I stabbed her again to silence her."

"Well, did it work? Did it silence her?"

"It silenced her…. Forever. Trust me man, I didn't kill her on purpose. This is the truth. I had to take away her life to save my own."

Inspector Hari walked in and asked, "Inspector Arvind, can you come out. I have some news for you."

Inspector Arvind obliged. Robin was alone in the room for five minutes. Then a doctor walked in. The doctor cleaned up his wounds. He also took his blood sample and hair sample. Robin was later asked to pee in a jar for further investigation. He also had to submit his fingerprints.

Inspector Hari informed Inspector Arvind that her body has been found and it has been taken for an autopsy.

The lodge was raided. Arrests were made at the lodge and they were interviewed.

A day passed by and Robin was still in the Police Station. Inspector Arvind and Inspector Hari hadn't slept for more than 24 hours.

Inspector Hari had a meeting with Inspector Arvind.

Inspector Hari asked Inspector Arvind, "Do you think he's telling the truth?"

"Yeah I think so. The cuts on his ankle were quite deep. The doctors who examined him said that they couldn't have been self inflicted. So I guess he did act in self defense."

"Yes, that's true."

"And the knife that was found on the crime scene had fingerprints of both Robin and Asha. So I guess that's it. He's telling the truth."

"Ya, but when we interviewed the people working at the lodge, they all said that they have never seen either of them."

"Obviously, they had to say it. They wouldn't want anything to do with a murder."

"Ya, that makes sense."

"So this is what we do, okay. We take Robin with us to the court. We'll get him a lawyer. We'll make Robin tell everything to the court. We'll try convincing the court that Asha killed Alan because he didn't pay her and he treated her miserably. So that's her motive. Now, I know that there's insufficient proof but we can plant some evidence. We'll play it our way. We'll see what we can do. The media will obviously eat up this story. 'A PROSTITUTE MURDERED HER CUSTOMER'. Headlines like that will get them high ratings. So they'll be happy with the way we end this case. And plus who's going to come in support of Asha anyways. She's a prostitute for God's sake. We did background checks on her which confirm that she doesn't have any friends or family. She can be framed easily. Nobody will come in her support. And plus she can't even defend herself. She's dead. The lawyer who will be representing her will be some clueless jackass. The court will be easily convinced that she killed Alan. If we close this case we can finally go to our homes and we'll probably get a medal. So let's end this case as soon as possible."

"Okay fine. I'm sure we'll be closing Alan's murder case very soon. But what about Asha's murder case?"

"See, I really feel that this boy is not guilty and he acted on self defense. But we'll leave that to the court. We'll just present all the evidence we have to the court and wait for the judgment. If the court finds Robin innocent then good, if they find him guilty then fine. How are we affected? We are just going to do everything possible to close the two cases and head home. That's it. And I have a feeling that these cases will be closed very soon."

"Oh great. And one more thing, Robin's lawyer has submitted his bail. Robin will be let out in two hours. But he won't be leaving town because he should be appearing in court next week."

"Good. Very good. Finally some progress."

An hour later the cops invite Robin's lawyer for tea and had a friendly chat with him.

Another hour later they gave Robin his possessions like his watch, phone etc. They asked him to sign a few papers and they let him loose.

Robin walked outside the police station and sighed.

And he thought to himself, "Phew, finally my journey back to normalcy has begun. Once this is over I can go back to living a normal life. And this time I'm not going to let my imaginary dad, stoned clouds or my own mind let me wander around again. I'm normal, I'm normal, I'm normal."

It was very cloudy that day and it began to drizzle.

As soon as he reached the gate of the police station someone from the back shouted, "Hey Robin, you forgot to collect your wallet."

When he turned around he saw Inspector Hari holding a black wallet.

Robin puts his hand into his back pocket and finds out that there's nothing there, "Shit I must've forgotten to collect my wallet."

As Robin turned to go and collect his wallet, Inspector Hari noticed a white piece of paper hanging out of the wallet. As he was holding the wallet upside down the piece of paper slipped and fell down.

Inspector Hari picked it up and asked, "Hey Robin, were you planning to go to Goa?"

Robin who was walking towards Inspector Hari now stopped his steps and asked nervously, "What? Goa?"

Inspector Hari looked at him suspiciously and said, "Yeah Goa, why did you buy a train ticket to Goa on the same day you killed Asha… for self defense. All the details are right here on the ticket, the date, the destination, your name, it's got everything. Is there something we need to know?"

"No, no inspector there's nothing else to be said." stuttered Robin who started to walk backwards who knew that they would find out about that train.

"Are you sure that you've nothing else to say? Because we will send our men to this train and find out everything." said Inspector Hari.

At that point Robin felt paranoid. He knew he was doomed. He knew that they would find out that he boarded the train and so did Ruchita. He knew they would eventually find out that he pulled her out of the train and killed her like a cold animal. Not knowing what to do he turned around and began to walk away.

"Hey, come back here? I have some new questions for you." shouted Inspector Hari.

By the time Inspector Hari finished his sentence Robin started running. Inspector Hari and two other cops started running after him yelling, "Come back."

Robin crossed the road and ran like a hungry mad dog. And the cops were right behind him, chasing him like a bunch of hyenas.

When Robin reached the end of the road he found a bridge that was under construction. The under constructed bridge could be climbed only by a small slippery ladder and no vehicles could get on that bridge. It was a bridge made for pedestrians to walk over railway tracks but one couldn't get to the other end of the bridge as it was under construction. He climbed the ladder and got on top of the bridge and looked down. Under the bridge were bright lights, red and blue shining from the police cars. There were at least ten cops and three police cars down there. He could hear the police dogs barking, the constables marching, and the TV reporters whining. He could see school children who stopped playing their cricket match because they wanted to come by and watch this since this was way more interesting. He could see old men looking up at Robin and wondering whether he'll ever reach their age.

He looked up and it was still drizzling. He looked down and noticed two cops trying to climb the bridge. When he realized that these cops would make it to the top of the bridge, he walked to the edge of the bridge; the dead end of the bridge. When he got to the dead end he leaned forward and noticed that there were railway tracks below the bridge.

The cops made it to the top of the bridge. With handcuffs on one side and death staring at him on another side Robin had to make a decision.

The road near the bridge got noisier as the number of police cars increased from three to six. Now there was even an ambulance and a fire truck along with the police cars.

By now six cops had made it to the top of the bridge.

It had stopped drizzling and had gotten sunny and bright all of a sudden.

The cops tried to calm the situation. They tried to calm the crowd, the reporters and most importantly Robin.

The six cops who got up didn't get too close to Robin. They were standing at a distance and one cop yelled at Robin, "Relax man. Just come back with us to the station and we'll talk. Nothing bad we'll happen."

Robin was standing at the edge of the under constructed bridge. He looked up and he couldn't see any clouds on the sunny blue sky. He thought to himself, "Wow! Where am I? What am I doing here? How did I end up here? Am I about to kill myself? I guess suicide runs in our family blood. Like dad, like son I guess. I've lived so many good days, I have had so many good memories from the past. If only I could return to normalcy. If only I could live some of those good old days again. I guess nobody can turn back time, now can they? The hands of the clock have slapped me hard. I wonder what my mother is doing right now. I wonder whether she is watching me on TV right now. I wonder what's going through her mind. She saw her husband die and now she'll watch her only son die. I wish I could see my mother's face one last time. She took such good care of me only to see me end up like this. I'm really going to miss my mother. What if I kill myself? Then what happens? Where do I go? What happens when my life ends? All those good simple childhood days, lunch time during school, bunking during college, drinking with my friends; all those times have been reduced to a memory that is stored in my mind. And now all those memories will be reduced to ashes. Are memories designed to fade? Where do they all go after they fade? I don't know why, but I feel that somewhere far, far away a memory is staring at me right now. Staring at me all confused and lost. And I'm staring back at it like I'm staring into a mirror. I wonder who will listen to the voice inside my head once I'm gone. I hope my mother forgives me for this."

As Robin stood there staring down at death one of the old police officers shouted, "Don't do it son, don't jump."

Robin looked back and shouted, "Don't come any closer to me or I'll jump. Stay away, stay right there."

The old man replied, "Okay we'll stand right here, we won't get any closer to you. But don't jump, let us talk to you."

Robin kept quiet for a while and said, "But you will arrest me. You'll tie my hands and throw me in jail for the rest of my life."

The old man smiled and replied, "I'm not sure. I don't know whether we'll put you in prison. And neither will you if you jump."

And that's when Robin thought to himself, "Hey, you know what? This man maybe right. How do I know my life is going to get worse if I don't live at all?"

He stood there silently for a good five minutes.

And then he opened his mouth and said slowly and softly, "If I die I'll never know. But I know one thing for sure. I know that it's best not to know. Because the more answers you find, the more questions arise. And I've already faced enough questions; life threatening questions, mind numbing questions, depressing demented questions. I'm tired of answers and questions old man. My time has come. Time has come for me to disappear like those stoned clouds. I've got to go now, got to go meet my father."

The old man stared back at him with a confused look on his face as did the other officers who heard Robin murmur those words.

He looked up at the sky and wondered, "In a way my Father, Alan, Ruchita were all my victims, I guess. And my last victim is me."

Robin took a step backwards.

He died.